SCAMMED

Ahmed Faiyaz grew up in Bangalore and now lives in Dubai. He's a strategist by profession, with a number of years in management consulting behind him. He is the bestselling author of *Love, Life and All That Jazz* and *Another Chance*. His stories are also featured in the bestselling Urban Shots series.

SCAMMED

Confessions
of a Confused
Accountant

AHMED FAIYAZ

RUPA

Rupa Publications India Pvt. Ltd 2014
7/16, Ansari Road, Daryaganj
New Delhi 110002

Sales Centres:

Allahabad Bengaluru Chennai
Hyderabad Jaipur Kathmandu
Kolkata Mumbai

Copyright © Ahmed Faiyaz 2011

First published in India by Grey Oak Publishers, 2011

ISBN: 978-81-291-3530-8

First impression 2014

10 9 8 7 6 5 4 3 2 1

The moral right of the author has been asserted.

Dedicated to

My mother—without whose support I would have remained a confused accountant. Thanks, Mom.

CHAPTER I

Hitesh walked hastily into the office, drenched from head to toe. The guard gave him an apathetic smile and returned to his work. Hitesh regretted not taking his raincoat when he'd left home; he hadn't expected a shower on this cool September evening. He removed his jacket, placed it beside his office bag, next to his desk, adjusted his clothes and walked towards the restroom. He waved cheerfully to the glum-faced flunkies who were still in office working like machines, on assignments of Sahil's clients, the way he had been doing for the last three years.

Today was the earliest that he would be getting home, he thought, looking at the big office clock that had just struck seven. Sahil Arora had called him to office to discuss his appraisal. Hitesh hoped he would finally hear some good news. He returned from the restroom and peeked inside Sahil's cabin. The man was typing away furiously on his laptop, looking serious and busy.

'Give me ten minutes, Hitesh. I'll call you,' Sahil said, without looking up.

'Okay, sir, I'll be at my desk.'

'Done.'

Hitesh went to his desk, turned on his computer and waited for Windows to load. He flipped through the pages of his self-appraisal form for the umpteenth time. Twenty assignments in the past year; clocking over 2,450 billable hours to clients; chargeability over 120 per cent. This might just be the day when he would become the manager, he thought. He turned around and stared longingly at the empty cubicle in the managers' area. A position had just become vacant, and to many he seemed to be the best person to fill that, given that Smith & Donald, a leading accounting and audit firm, had a preference to promote home-grown talent—people who stayed with the firm for a while.

His experience with the firm now added up to seven years; four years as a trainee, and the rest since he had qualified as an accountant. He was last promoted eighteen months ago, unlike Sahil, who had started his career in the firm with him, but had moved far ahead. Sahil had managed to qualify a year before Hitesh and, since then, had been promoted every year. He was now a senior manager, one of the three that the firm had in the Hyderabad office. And now he was set to become a partner in the coming three or four years, even before he turned thirty-five. Hitesh was reduced to Sahil's go-to man, who worked on most of his assignments, managing limited resources and delivering on stiff deadlines.

A colleague walked up to Hitesh. 'How are things, sir?' he asked.

'All well, Ashutosh. How are you? Which assignment are you working on?' Hitesh asked.

'This one is painful, sir. United Cables, your old client. That joker, Ramdorai, is making my life miserable.'

'I think the books are in a mess. To top it all, he's a difficult person to deal with,' Hitesh said, smiling sympathetically.

'I can't wait to finish this and go on my examination leave. I still have one group remaining…'

'November isn't far,' Hitesh interrupted. 'I hope your in-charge for the assignment is giving you time to study.'

'Supriya?' Ashutosh sniggered. 'She passes the office time either chatting on the phone or doing her nails. As usual, it is me who is doing all the work. If she had her way, I'd be even chopping vegetables in her kitchen.'

Hitesh laughed. 'You haven't had your appraisal yet, right? Don't worry. I am sure you'll pass this time,' he said reassuringly.

'I wish, sir. But what can one say about these appraisals? This whole 360 degrees feedback policy is nothing but a sham. In fact, it is more like 360 degrees ass-kissing,' Ashutosh said with a sad smile. 'Whatever it is, I'm not bothered. All I want is to pass my examination, and put in my papers the very next day.'

'Oh, is it? What are your plans? Where will you go then?'

'My brother is in London, sir. He is trying to find me a job there. Once I clear my exams, it would be easier. Anyway, did you hear who is going to fill that seat?' Ashutosh gestured to the empty cubicle.

'God knows. But I hope it's me,' said Hitesh, more to himself.

He pushed his hair back and suddenly had a good feeling about his upcoming meeting.

'You haven't heard, then. It is Supriya who is being promoted to fill the position. I heard her on the phone; she was gushing with ecstasy when people called up to wish her. Tomorrow the office mail will also go out,' Ashutosh retorted, while Hitesh stood baffled and stunned.

'But she joined just six months ago…'

'Sir, your boss is very fond of her. He even comes over to the client's office to pay a visit when she's around. A lot has been happening over lunch and coffee,' Ashutosh said with a wink. 'Anyway, let me finish and leave. I need to study. Good luck, sir.'

'Thank you. But this is…surprising,' Hitesh muttered. Crestfallen, he walked back to his desk and signed into his personal email account. Following his daily ritual for the past one year, he browsed through the job openings in the job search portal. In the last few months, he had attended a few interviews and received a couple of offers. But he was waiting for a bigger and better opportunity. His desk phone buzzed: it was from the boss' cabin.

'Come fast,' Sahil said, before hanging up hastily. Hitesh picked up a heap of papers, including his appraisal form and the notes that he had made on assignments he had done so far.

'How is the Ventura Software assignment going?' Sahil asked, revolving in his chair to face him. He looked smart, dressed in a Tommy Hilfiger shirt and a Zodiac tie.

'We have a lot of outstanding requests for information. We're trying to...' Hitesh began, looking distracted.

'Get it done fast. There's another important assignment that's come up. I need you to leave for Vizag next week. Wrap this up by the weekend.'

'Sahil, it isn't that easy. We have a lot of findings. Working papers need to be documented properly. I don't have the best staff with me. I need at least a week more.'

'No way! Supreme Motors has to begin next week and finish in a month. Push it, finish kar yaar, salta de.'

'Hmm...Can we discuss the appraisal?' Hitesh asked trying to not sound too irritated.

'Yes, of course! Is this your self-appraisal form?' Sahil asked, taking the papers from him. He flipped through the pages and chuckled while reading some of Hitesh's comments in the boxes. He quickly entered his ratings in the applicable boxes and finished up with a stylish signature with his Cross pen.

'Have a look at it, and if you're okay with it, I'll send it off to HR in the morning.' Sahil sat back in his chair and hummed softly to himself, while Hitesh went through the form. In the meanwhile, Sahil picked up his phone and typed on his keypad, noticing Hitesh's expression change from hopeful to irritated from the corner of his eye.

An annoyed Hitesh scratched his head and looked up. 'Can you tell me why I have been rated 2.5 out of five? As per my rating, it should be 3.5.'

'I can't give everyone what they feel they should get, can I?' Sahil grinned.

'Well, I don't believe this is fair, and I cannot accept it,' an exasperated Hitesh said.

'See, Hitesh, you are making it difficult for me. You're a friend. Tell me, how do I do that? Look at my ratings; I've kept those the same as yours in eight out of the ten boxes. Only in team work and personality you've gone down. What can I do? This is based on feedback.'

'What feedback?'

'You refused to take on some of Anita Rao's work while you were doing the DSK Bank assignment. She gave a feedback about you that you weren't supportive.'

'She had very little work and even that she couldn't finish! Why should I take on everything? You know how many hours I spend at work; that girl walks out at six!'

'She is the partner's niece. You should have been more careful. The feedback went right to the top. Anyway, it was an important assignment; there should have been better teamwork. The partner thinks that you aren't a team player.'

'I don't agree. I've done twenty assignments in a year. Who else…'

'And another: your personality. You need to smarten up,' Sahil said, looking straight into Hitesh's eyes, while Hitesh went red in the face. 'You wear red shirts and maroon ties to work. Learn to dress soberly. Look a little more professional.'

'Is this what the appraisal is about?'

'It isn't just that. You were on an office trip recently; you insisted on some old '70's music being played in the bus. People are still laughing at your snake dance.'

'Those were some great numbers by Kishore Kumar. Sahil, please be fair. Appraise me on my work.'

'I am, and this is what the partner tells me when I talk about your promotion. Supriya thinks you're anti-social. You don't mix around and dress and dance funny. You even threw a fit during the office lunch when there was no vegetarian food. Learn to adjust, yaar.'

'So what? What if I don't want to socialize with her? I don't drink alcohol and eat everything that you people do. I just cannot believe this. Are these the reasons that are pulling my rating down?'

'See, friend. You're a hard-working guy and a good resource. But there are things that need a lot of improvement.'

'Does this mean that I'm not getting promoted?' Hitesh asked, throwing his hands up in frustration.

'No. But we will have to wait until we see that you are manager material. See, this long hair and the lime-green shirt with the green tie...'

'Well, I'll quit then. If I'm not worthy enough to be promoted, I'll quit,' Hitesh snapped. He was in a combative mood, outraged at the way he was being treated.

'Chill, yaar. You're doing well. Who says you're not? Give it some time. My hands are tied this time. We could promote only one person and Supriya had better acceptance. Let's give it six months, maybe I can push...'

'Sahil, I joined this firm with you, and I've done every assignment to the best of my capability. Why am I being held back? This just isn't fair when people who come from outside become managers in six months.'

Sahil looked shifty and averted his gaze from Hitesh.

'See, I can't promote you and I don't want you to leave. I'll do something for you as a friend. I'll promote you to deputy manager with a ten per cent pay hike. This is the most I can do in this situation. I'm creating a position to accommodate you!'

'Is this a promotion?'

'Of course! And, in six months, we can try to make you manager. Maybe earlier, if someone quits,' Sahil said, looking at his phone screen and smiling at a message he had just received.

'What choice do I have?' asked Hitesh, face creased in anger.

'Take it up. It's good for you. Not what you wanted, but still a promotion. I'll change the rating to 2.9. That's the most I can do. You know I've always looked after you as a friend.' Hitesh couldn't recollect a single instance when he had been looked after. He was just an overworked mule in the firm whom people poked jokes at him for his dressing sense and dancing style.

'Okay, let me think about it. I'll come back to you,' Hitesh said, staring at the papers in his hand.

'Let's finish this now, as I need to send the email to Delhi. They'll be emailing all our offices the names of those who've been promoted.'

'But you're saying in six months things will change, right?'

'We can try,' Sahil said, looking impatiently at his watch. 'Look, let's really finish this and leave. Supriya and I are going over to the partner's place for dinner and drinks. I'm also playing golf with him on the weekend and I'll put in a good word for you then.'

'You and Supriya are going over to Sundar's house for dinner!'

'Yes, yaar, we've been invited there for a get-together. Smarten up, man; you must learn how to network,' he said, as he put on his blazer and turned down the screen of his laptop. 'Aur yaar, ease off the job search portals. Focus on finishing the assignment quickly. You have to go to Vizag for the Supreme Motors audit and you'll have Sandra to accompany you. Hopefully you'll be a good team player this time,' Sahil said and looked up with a wink.

A despondent Hitesh walked back to his cubicle and shut down his computer. Picking up his helmet, bag and the still wet jacket, he walked out and went towards the area where his motorcycle was parked, and saw Sahil zipping away in his Ford Fiesta.

When he reached home, he found his parents waiting for him with expectant eyes.

'Will you have poori or chappati?' his mother asked.

'I'm not hungry, Ma,' Hitesh said, dropping his bag on the floor and sitting down.

His father, who was now browsing through news channels, turned towards him after reducing the volume from a deafening high. 'What happened to the appraisal?' he asked.

'I got promoted,' Hitesh replied with a slight smile.

'Oh, that's great!' his mother rushed to hug him. Her eyes beamed with joy; she had been waiting for this moment for long.

'Good. After all the slogging, they have finally made you a manager,' his father exclaimed, nodding his head in appreciation.

'Err, no. Not exactly...' Hitesh began.

'What then?' asked his father suspiciously, leaning forward as Hitesh sank back in his chair and his stodgy mother stood before him, with hands on her hips.

'Papa, they made me a deputy manager.'

'You said they promoted you.'

'Yes,' Hitesh said, turning to face his mother, who looked confused.

'Aren't you an assistant manager now?' she asked.

'Yes, what is the difference? To me it sounds like the same thing,' chimed in his father, sounding angry and scratching the scanty hair on his head.

'It isn't. In six months, there's a chance for another promotion.'

'Rubbish! You are a fool,' his father said, loosening the top button of his shirt and burping loudly.

'You studied for so many years and still aren't doing well. Kanchal got married to a banker in the US. Kantaben's daughter, Hemal, has got engaged to the vice-president of wealth management in a big bank in Mumbai. Your father is just a small-time jeweller; for us, finding you a match is very difficult. What would we say? My son is a deputy manager, tch.' She shook her head dismissively.

'Ma, I'm not interested in this conversation. I am tired and want to go and sleep. I need to finish my work here in a week. Next week, I have to travel.'

'What about pay hike? How much?' asked his father with expectant eyes.

'Ten per cent, Papa,' Hitesh answered with some hesitation.

'Useless! Inflation itself is more than eleven per cent. Those fellows in call centres these days make more than you. You have to pay taxes also. Find another job,' he said with a scowl.

'Why don't you try in the US, beta? Your cousin Jignesh is also working there. Look at the amount of jewellery your aunty buys. They also bought a new Honda car recently. What do we have? Your Papa's old Zen,' his mother said politely, ruffling his hair. 'Should I get you some buttermilk?'

Hitesh shook his head. His mind was busy figuring out how to finish the impossible assignment in three days, before he travelled the following week. *This weekend is also gone*, he thought. *That bastard Sahil must be having fun.*

'Don't trust that Sahil fellow. He's not going to promote you. No,' his father gesticulated, before he belched loudly and watched Hitesh leave the room.

Little did Hitesh know that the Vizag trip was going to turn the tables altogether, and life would never be the same for him in six months from the day of his appraisal.

CHAPTER 2

Two weeks later

'Mr Varun, it's important that I have confirmations from your dealers in the North on sales made to them. It's hard to believe that sales in the last quarter of the year account for more than fifty per cent of your annual sales,' Hitesh said pensively, as the balding Varun Rao, sales manager at Supreme Motors, scratched his head.

'Last year too we didn't give any confirmations to the auditor. We are telling you, no? The sale is done; finished. Why should we bother our dealers with constant requests for something that is done and over? No, not good,' he said, a little irritated.

'Mr Varun, we have to ensure that what is recorded in the books is true and correct. I request you to kindly cooperate…'

'See, I have a lot of things to do: challans to fill, sales documentation to be completed. I need to go. I have given you what Mehta Sir had requested. Rest you ask him, no? After all, he is the CFO,' Mr Varun said defiantly and tapped on the table.

'We request you to get us the confirmations…' Hitesh persisted.

'Arey, what confirmations? I will talk to Mehta sir. I don't have time for this. This is an audit, not some CID investigation,' he said with a raised pitch, before he got up and walked out of the cabin in a huff.

Moments later, one of the accountants, Naresh, walked in. He was the only member of the management at the plant who cooperated with Hitesh.

'Naresh, I want the names of employees on the rolls to be tallied with those living in the housing society. I learn that we have 450 employees but 650 fully occupied housing units. Why is this?' Hitesh asked.

'I don't know, sir. I…I will get you the file after talking to Mehta sir,' Naresh replied nervously and left the cabin.

Hitesh shook his head with worry. The books were in a mess, and he had received little cooperation from any of the managers at the Supreme Motors plant. He realised that the company was run by old-time crooks, each of whom had their own vested interests. Mehta, the CFO, operated out of Hyderabad and had refused to come to Visakhapatnam, despite the fact that the audit was underway. He had heard stories about how Mehta was attacked by an angry mob when a major layoff happened at the plant, a couple of years ago. To Hitesh, nothing seemed to add up: the expenses were on a rise, the cash situation was precarious, sales seemed unrealistic, and a profit was shown in the company's books, which was actually the result of sale of land for a shopping complex.

His phone rang and he picked it up, feeling annoyed. 'Tell me, Ma,' he said as he browsed through the file before him.

'Arey Hitu, what should I do for you? I tried so hard to convince Divya's family but they don't want her to marry you. She is an HR manager in a big software company, the Windows one…'

'Microsoft, Ma.' Hitesh grew irritated. *Thank God,* he thought.

'Oh yes, that one. They said you are just an assistant manager, while she is a manager. She is also four years younger…'

'Ma, thanks for telling me this. But I really need to work. I'm hanging up, bye,' he said and disconnected the call.

It rang again. This time it was Sahil. 'Tell me, sir,' Hitesh said, sounding tired.

'What's going on, boss? I hear you're behaving like the angry young man Amitabh Bachchan of the '70s. What are you up to?'

'Just doing my work, sir; using the methods we should use, requesting for the information we need to see…'

'Boss, the client is getting angry. I just got a call from Mehta, who rudely interrupted my lunch with Supriya. He says you're running some kind of fraud investigation there; all his managers are complaining to him. He wanted to talk to the partner.'

'Sahil, I need the evidence…'

'So you are indeed running an investigation. Boss, the partner went to school with the owner of Supreme Motors. This is an important client. Stop fucking things up! Close out, yaar! I want you to finish your work at the plant by this weekend.'

'Sahil, I can't. Sandra hasn't come to office today. She was ill yesterday too. Some stomach infection it is. I'm covering up her work too…'

'Can't help it, yaar. I want this project closed out. Your allocated time on this finishes this week. I want a hundred per cent chargeability!'

'Boss, things are in a mess. It isn't that easy.'

'Yaar, you want to become a manager, right? Wrap it up. I want no further issues,' Sahil said curtly before hanging up.

'They're all the same,' a voice said and Hitesh looked up. It was Naresh, standing before him with a file. Hitesh hadn't noticed him enter the cabin. 'It's a bloody pain,' Hitesh responded dejectedly.

'I know what you mean. Hitesh, meet me this evening at Tasty Bites Café. It's located at the other end of the city, a safe place to sit and talk. I'll tell you all about what is really going on here,' he said softly, handing him the file and walking out.

∎

Hitesh walked into the cramped café after he had paid off the autorickshaw driver. Naresh was already inside, waiting for him, a nervous expression on his face.

'I've just ordered some snacks and coffee for both of us,' he said as he saw Hitesh.

'Thanks. I need to go back soon and work in the night on this file,' Hitesh spoke in a tired voice.

'No point, boss. All the slogging makes little sense here. The only thing that works in this company is power. I did my M.Com, and this was the only job I could get then.' Naresh sighed and continued, 'You are not aware of the level of corruption out here. Tell me, did you change autos at the bazaar like I asked you to?'

'Yes I did. But what's going on?' Hitesh asked, curious.

'I have collected some evidence. Take it to the management. See if they can do anything about it.'

'What kind of evidence?' Hitesh rolled up his sleeves.

'Do you know R.V. Suresh, our purchase manager?' asked Naresh, taking a sip of coffee.

'Yes, how can I forget him? His blood pressure shot up when I queried him. He even shouted at me to leave his cabin,' Hitesh said.

'Well, here's an analysis of the top fifty items of purchase made by the company, in the past one year,' Naresh said, handing Hitesh a sheet. 'Listed on it is the price per unit we paid versus the market price, averaged from three vendors in the business for each of the items.'

Hitesh read the tables on the printed sheet with an exasperated look.

'You'll see that we've, on an average, paid thirty to forty per cent more on each of the items…' Naresh began.

'But isn't there a process of tendering? I've seen some of the bidding paperwork…' Hitesh interrupted.

'Yes, there is, and it allows only the bidders pre-qualified by Suresh's department. You'll see that he's pre-qualified only five firms for these items of frequent purchase. Look into these firms' background: you'll find nothing. The only company they deal with is Supreme Motors. I've found out that Raj Trading, International Motors & Spares and South Vizag Spare Parts are firms owned by him and his family.'

'You don't say! Saala!' a nonplussed Hitesh exclaimed.

'And one of the firms is owned by a group of employees in his department. All the stationery, toners, etc. come from them. His father-in-law has the contract to run the grocery store in the housing complex.'

'This is crazy! How can he get away with all this?'

'Hitesh, all the other managers are involved. Decisions on key items of purchase are taken by a committee that comprises of all the crooks. Everyone takes a share. No wonder Suresh lives in a huge apartment and goes on holidays to Singapore and Dubai.'

'What about the rest?' a worried Hitesh asked.

'Varun Rao, whom you had an argument with today, is another crook. Cars with manufacturing defects are auctioned off by the company. Often, these defects are deliberate. He buys these at the auction for thirty per cent of the price, gets them fixed at the company free of cost, and his brother sells the cars at double the price he buys these at.'

'Yes, I noticed a more than ten per cent defect rate every year. I wondered how it could be so high.'

'Well, here are the papers. His firm, fronted by his wife, has bought about fifty cars every year, and he's made a killing. The sales numbers he shows at the end of every year are false. Here is the documentation. None of these dealers in the North exist anymore; they shut down over ten years ago. He shows entries on paper and adjusts for returns in the following year. It's the same scam every year'

'Where does the HR manager, G.V. Vinod, feature in all this?'

'You asked me about the housing complex this morning. Most of those units are illegally let out to businesses and people working outside. When we retrenched people two years ago, he let them stay on at a rent he receives directly. Some were let out to outsiders. My cousin is a tenant and pays 2,000 rupees a month.'

'This is a huge amount, if you consider about 200 to 250 units let out this way!' Hitesh said with his brows raised.

'It is. And I hear he plans to increase the rent this year. A lot of those who didn't get fired and stayed had to make a little payment under the table. At least fifty of the employees on the books today are people who don't work here anymore or have long been deceased, but the salary continues to be given to them. Some of this is political too…'

'I'm sure,' Hitesh said, nodding his head. 'What does Mohan Babu have to do with this?'

'He's the boss, the kingpin; the head of production and the de-facto in-charge of the company. I hear he gets a standard thirty per cent cut out of what each of these guys make. He controls things and people who can make noise. The political clout he has can't be ignored. He was a union leader who rose to his current position; I hear that he will stand for elections in two years. If he gets elected, and if his party wins, I hear he'll be made a minister.'

'And these people will keep flogging the dead horse, which is this company. Do Venugopal Reddy and Mehta have any idea about all this?'

'Some idea, not the whole of it. You can show them the complete picture. See, they want the company to survive too. It was their flagship for many years, and Venugopal has put money into films and real estate. These investments are yet to yield dividends. They have some sense of who they're dealing with. But these papers could help shake things up a bit.'

'Will you be safe? What if they trace back the source of this information?'

'Hitesh, I am not that foolish. My parents have already moved to Muscat. I leave with my wife and son tomorrow morning. I'll be safe. See what you can do. As I see it, these guys are making money while the poor are getting exploited. This company can't last for more than a year, at the rate at which they're burning cash.'

'I know. Nobody is buying these cars today, and you can't sell land every year and show a profit.'

'That's exactly what they're planning. They are selling a parcel of land to a politician, which they plan to develop into residential property. There are 400 cars lying at dealerships that may be in a poor condition, and these will come back to the company now or in the near future. Yet we continue production, as it is profitable for some people to continue the racket.'

'How long can they do this? It's a tough situation. In a year, there would be a lot of people who would be out of work.' Hitesh sat back with a worried look on his face.

'I know and I leave it to you. I need to rush now; we have to board a train to Hyderabad tonight and then a flight tomorrow morning. Good luck,' Naresh said as he stood up and rushed out of the café, leaving the table strewn with papers of evidence he had collected.

■

Hitesh paid the autorickshaw driver and walked into the narrow lane. At the end of the lane was the company guest house where he and Sandra were put up. He had carefully tucked away the papers handed over by Naresh in his office bag. He tried to imagine what reactions the revelations about the corrupt managers at the plant would provoke. He hoped Sandra would come to office the next day so that he could quickly wrap up the work and leave for Hyderabad.

'Hitesh Babu,' someone hollered to him. He turned to find it was the rotund G.V. Vinod, leaning against the bonnet of a grey Supreme Pride.

'Oh…Mr Vinod, I was startled for a moment. How are you?' Hitesh said, trying to hide his nervousness.

'All okay; we have been waiting for you for a long time,' he said, putting his hand over his tummy.

'Busy roaming around, huh?' said another voice. Hitesh saw it was R.V. Suresh, who was stepping out of the car from the driver's seat.

'Er...no; just sightseeing a bit of the city.'

'Not much to see. Is there, Vinod Garu?' Suresh asked, eyes fixed on Hitesh.

'Yes nothing. Only shops and hotels,' Vinod guffawed. 'Have you taken your dinner yet?' he asked.

'No, I...'

'Good. We've come to pick you up. Mohan Babu and Varun Rao are waiting for us at the bar at Sea Shore President.'

'Really? I don't think I want to...'

'Come on, Hitesh Babu. Let's hurry up,' Vinod said, opening the door for him. Hitesh got in reluctantly. They started the car and sped away. On the way, Hitesh noticed the car's interiors which gave him an unpleasant feeling about the owner. A mafia don's car wouldn't be much different from this, he imagined. The seats had fur as an upholstery cover; a whiff of burnt incense sticks pervaded the interior; a picture of a popular South Indian actress in a wet swimsuit was stuck on the windscreen; and the windows were tinted dark. The three spoke little during the short drive.

The car stopped and the three stepped out. 'This is a top-class hotel,' Vinod said, slapping Hitesh's back.

'Yes, you'll enjoy here,' Suresh winked at him. He lit up a Charminar and walked ahead.

Heading up from the reception, they walked past a couple of dangerous-looking bouncers into a dingy pub. It was filled with smoke, and was sparsely lit, apart from green and purple disco lights that flickered every few seconds. Hindi music from the '90s blared out of the speakers.

The three of them took their seats at the end of the bar, where the other two men sat waiting. Varun Rao had bloodshot eyes and was quickly downing his whisky, while Mohan Babu sat with a grimace, scratching his head.

'Come, come Hitesh Garu, sit with me. Welcome!' Mohan Babu said, taking Hitesh's hand and shaking it furiously.

'Good evening,' Hitesh said uneasily. Varun Rao held up his glass and nodded to him. Suresh and Vinod called out to the waiter.

'See, we have not had a good relationship with you so far. Varun, Suresh and you have had arguments I've been told about. I apologize to you; we should be friends. After all, you're here to help us,' Mohan Babu said, fixing his gaze at Hitesh while Varun Rao looked on, disinterested.

'Yes, you're helping the company. We want our company to be the best,' Vinod added, rather foolishly, while Suresh cleared his throat.

'We should cooperate and work together,' butted in Varun, in what Hitesh felt was not much of a friendly voice, pointing to Hitesh and glaring at him with disdain, while Suresh blew smoke in his direction.

'How is that girl, saar? We hear she is unwell and not coming to office,' said Mohan Babu, scratching his head.

Hitesh loosened his tie and sat back. 'I'm afraid she's been down with a bout of flu,' he said, trying to sound confident.

'Oh, is that so?' Mohan Babu said, smiling and nodding his head, and averting his gaze to Suresh, who grinned like a monkey.

'If you don't mind, watch this.' Vinod said, carefully handing Hitesh his sleek mobile phone.

Hitesh looked at the screen and was taken aback. The screen showed a picture of Sandra kissing a man. 'Scroll to your left,' Vinod continued, tapping on the table.

Hitesh scrolled through a number of images of Sandra and the man drinking, making out and laughing together. He found them repulsive and stopped scrolling further.

'So you have been spying on the employees of our company?' Hitesh asked, trying to hide his anger.

'Oh no, no. No. It is the caretaker of the guest house who is telling everybody that a boy from Hyderabad visits this madam daily, and they both have fun. We had heard from you that she is unwell. We were curious, you know. So we just asked him to prove it. That's all,' Vinod said, flustered, but coaxing a smile.

'Rama. Tch tch…Indecent. Very shameful!' Mohan Babu pretended, nodding his head.

Vinod felt better. 'We wanted to send this to your HR but then we thought she is a young girl, it might spoil her career. We just felt you should know,' he said, grabbing his phone back from Hitesh, who still looked shocked.

'What saar, Hitesh? You're working twenty-four hours a day and your junior is partying away to glory. If I were in your place, I wouldn't be killing myself with so much work,' Suresh said, nudging Varun Rao, who looked at Hitesh with contempt and snorted.

'What will you drink?' Mohan Babu broke in.

'I don't take liquor.'

Varun laughed. 'What a fellow! What do you drink then? Sir, have a brandy, for our friendship's sake,' Varun needled him, smiling wickedly.

'No, it's okay. Maybe a soft drink. Thums Up will do,' Hitesh said.

'Aye, waiter. Get a glass of milk…Oh sorry, one Thums Up,' Suresh shouted out to the waiter, who looked confused while the others grinned.

'Good one,' Varun said smiling. 'So… Haven't you done anything with this Sandra yet? How is she, boss? Send her to me. I'll *fully* cooperate,' he added. Hitesh looked disgusted and turned his face away.

'Stop it now, Varun. Poor Hitesh is embarrassed,' Mohan Babu said, smiling.

'Yes, he is a straight fellow. Decent,' Vinod said, pointing at Hitesh, while Suresh continued to smoke, with a sheepish smile plastered on his face.

'When is Lata coming over?' Suresh asked, moving away from the earlier conversation. He turned to Hitesh, who was nervously sipping his drink. 'Do you know that Lata is performing tonight?'

'Lata Mangeshkar? Here!' a dumbfounded Hitesh asked.

'Who?' Mohan Babu asked with a confused look on his face while the others laughed.

Suresh took a drag and grinned at him. 'You do have a sense of humour. This one is a local dancer. Superb item. A hot body like Bipasha Basu,' he said, nudging Varun Rao.

'Oh...okay,' Hitesh said and gulped his drink. The lights went out and flashed again.

A young, buxom woman clad in a see-through sari began gyrating to 'Ek, do, teen...' as the audience clapped and gaped at her, spellbound. Mohan Babu flared his nostrils and leaned in, as if in a trance, as the woman shook her body suggestively. Hitesh watched for a while, then turned his gaze away, wondering what to do.

The lewd performance ended and was followed by an awkward silence. The four quietly downed another round of drinks. Suddenly, Suresh got up and walked towards the back of the bar. He returned in a few minutes, grinning and looking satisfied.

'Done, sir. It's fixed. You can leave with her in fifteen minutes,' he casually told Mohan Babu and returned to his drink. Mohan Babu patted Suresh's back, his eyes shining with excitement. Hitesh cringed and shifted in his chair.

He opened his mouth to take his leave when Mohan Babu motioned to him to remain seated. 'I want to tell you a story before we leave,' he said, taking a drag from Suresh's cigarette, and watching Hitesh closely from the corner of his eye.

'Yes,' a tired Hitesh muttered.

'There was this fellow at the factory a year ago; a young manager, of about your age. He would constantly fight with me to streamline production, reduce defects...'

'Good intentions,' Vinod chimed in.

'But not practical,' Suresh added, shaking his head, grimacing and peering at Hitesh.

'He was being really difficult. One day he told me he'd show some reports to the management. I didn't know what reports, did I?' Mohan Babu turned to Suresh who shook his head. 'I didn't,' he continued, 'I told him "Go, babu. What can I do?" Mohan Babu looked at Vinod who answered, 'Of course'. 'Next day, the boy was to leave Vizag but, early in the morning, he went and jumped into the well.' Mohan Babu looked straight into Hitesh's eyes who looked stoned. 'Suicide,' Mohan Babu added, feigning sadness and shrugging his shoulders.

'Mad fellow,' Varun said, showing his betel-stained teeth.

'Foolish,' Suresh added.

An awkward moment passed. 'Sir, here she is. Time to go, sir,' Suresh suddenly said to Mohan Babu, who heaved himself up excitedly.

'We still let his family stay in the housing complex. Poor fellow,' Vinod said to Hitesh and got up too.

'Good to meet you, sir. We understand each other now. We are friends,' Mohan Babu proclaimed as a worried Hitesh nodded. He took Hitesh's bony hand and squeezed it.

'You are a very intelligent, capable young man,' Vinod said as Mohan Babu waved and walked away. The woman, her face caked in make-up, followed him out, holding the seams of her garish sari with one hand.

'You have a bright future,' Varun continued, popping some roasted peanuts in his mouth. 'You should tell that Sandra that her job lies in your hands. Who knows, it might work for you.'

'Let's go. Come, Hitesh Garu,' Vinod finally said. Hitesh got up quietly and followed him out of the bar, holding on to his office bag tightly. He badly needed some rest. He had seen more than enough for a day.

CHAPTER 3

Hitesh knocked on Sandra's door impatiently. He was dressed up and ready to leave for the factory, but had heard nothing from her. She hadn't even responded to his message last night asking whether she would be coming to work.

The door opened and Hitesh saw Sandra wearing loose trousers and a T-shirt, hair dishevelled and eyes groggy. 'Sorry, I'm still really unwell,' she moaned.

'Sandra, this "not well" act needs to stop. I know what goes on here during the day and so does the senior management at the factory. You should thank me for preventing a call being made to the partner.'

Sandra stood petrified. 'I'm sorry,' she muttered. 'Please don't complain about me, Hitesh. I beg of you.'

'Sandra, get ready. We're running late. I'll be waiting in my room. Fifteen minutes.'

'Okay,' she replied hastily, a little relieved.

Twenty minutes later, she appeared at his door, dressed in tight-fitted clothes and smelling of a strong perfume.

Hitesh was distracted but got up to leave. Sandra closed the door behind her and sat beside him. She put her hands around his neck and made an innocent face, as if about to cry. 'I broke up with my boyfriend last night. He'd been very difficult, showing up here unannounced and not letting me work, unlike you, so understanding and supportive.' She batted her eyelashes and snuggled closer to Hitesh while he hesitated.

'You're not going to complain about me, are you? Let's finish work, and go out for a movie,' she cooed, bringing her lips close to his and kissing him softly. Hitesh was surprised but enjoyed the attention nonetheless.

Half-dazed and half-worried, he stood up awkwardly. 'Hmm… Let's leave now. We're getting late,' he mumbled and walked towards the door.

'Yes, boss,' she said, rushing and taking his hand in hers.

CHAPTER 4

'Yes, Ma. Tell me,' Hitesh said, holding the phone between his ear and the shoulder as his fingers typed away on the keyboard, eyes fixed on the monitor.

'Hitu, you're on Raj Bhavan road, na?'

'Yes. Why?' Hitesh sounded much preoccupied as Sandra looked at him from her seat. The two were busy completing the Supreme Motors assignment at their head office in Hyderabad.

'Good. Dimple is meeting you for lunch at Minerva Coffee Shop. Be there at one. Rajat Mama is emailing you her photos right now. Check your computer.'

'Ma, what is this? I am tied up, and have no time to spare. We need to wind up…'

'Arey, she is very good. Working too. Nice family,' his mother prodded him. 'You please go. It's with a great difficulty that we've found a rishta for you,' she added, sounding annoyed.

Hitesh didn't want to argue with her in Sandra's presence. 'Yes, I will go for lunch,' he said softly and hung up. He turned towards Sandra and found her looking at him expectantly. They had planned to order pizza for lunch together. 'My mother wants me to meet an uncle over lunch. He's come down from Ahmedabad. I have to go, sorry,' he said, hesitantly, and quickly turned his eyes towards the monitor. Sensing Sandra was looking elsewhere, he click-opened the photos of Dimple. The girl seemed pretty and simple, dressed in Indian clothes in all the photos, apparently shot in a studio. He smiled to himself, and logged out of his computer.

'Alright. I'll order something for myself then,' Sandra said as he got up.

'Yes, please do. And finish up on your working papers. I want to review them once I'm back.'

'Yes boss,' she replied curtly, without looking up. Hitesh could sense she was upset, but decided against offering an explanation. He was still undecided about the status of their relationship. Though they had been spending a lot of time together since their return from Vizag, they were not officially a couple. Attention from a woman, that too from a stunner like Sandra, was totally new to Hitesh and he still couldn't believe his luck. But he revelled in this newfound bliss nonetheless, trying to erase from his mind the images of her making out with another guy.

He quietly walked out of the cabin towards the elevator.

∎

Hitesh sat waiting in the coffee shop, nervous and constantly checking his watch. He wondered if Dimple had the right address. He had to reach the client's office in an hour and attend a spate of meetings. And then there was Sandra. Was she angry with him? He thought about their dinner late last night, the coffee at the Taj Krishna and the ride back to her place. Suddenly, he looked up and saw a chubbier version of the girl in the pictures standing before him.

'Hi,' Dimple smiled nervously. She was wearing a bright red salwaar-kameez and almost a dozen bangles in each hand. Her face had layers of make-up, and some of the lipstick had made it to her teeth. Hitesh immediately found her repulsive.

'Hello,' he said calmly.

'Sorry yaar. I'm new in your city. The rickshaw driver took me around in circles.'

'It's okay. What will you eat? A vegetarian meal?'

'Yes, order that only.'

After Hitesh had placed the order, she gazed at him coyly, while he wondered how to end this amicably.

'You look very dashing. Just like in the photos,' she gushed.

'You too,' he said and turned his eyes away.

'When is your birthday?'

'Third of April.'

'Oh, Aries! Rani Mukherjee is also Aries. My favourite actor! You missed April Fool's Day by two days,' she said and giggled. 'People with your star sign are known to be courageous and good leaders. I read this in a newspaper.'

'Yes, I have heard that, too. I was born on the same day as Marlon Brando.'

'Who? A cricketer? Never heard of him.'

'No. He's an actor in Hollywood. You must have heard of *Godfather*,' he said and began gobbling up his food.

'No. I don't watch many English films. I last saw *Bunty aur Babli*. Too good. Fultoo time pass!' she grinned again.

'Okay. So what else do you do in your pastime?' Hitesh asked, not really wanting an answer.

'I reach home only at seven from office,' she said, making a face at him. 'I watch *Kasauti Life Ki* from eight to nine, and then *The Indian Dance Circus* from nine to ten. Fultoo masti it is! You know, I auditioned for *Dance Dhamaka* once, but they didn't take me.'

'Oh, is it? Why? I'm sure you must be good.'

'Yes. But they only want girls with a flat stomach. I've joined a gym now.'

'Okay…' Hitesh wondered where to look.

'What do you watch?'

'I don't watch much television. No time for that. When I do, it's mainly business news channels and old English films.'

'I love Charlie Chaplin films too. Fultoo comedy! He is so funny,' she said, laughing hysterically while her bangles jingled.

'Where do you work?'

'I take customer calls for Axis Car Rentals. We are doing very well. We have a fleet of two hundred cars in Hyderabad alone,' she said proudly.

'Yes, I've heard about the company. It was set up recently, wasn't it?'

'Yes. It's a subsidiary of Kansas Motors. They are a large automobile company. So all our cars are from Kansas Motors...'

'Hmm...Good idea to sell cars: start a car rental company,' Hitesh interrupted.

'Whatever. What are your hobbies?'

'I used to play chess and table tennis a lot at the YMCA. Now I don't get enough time. I watch old English and Hindi films on the weekend.'

'Me too. I watch TV all day on weekends. MTV is fultoo time pass. But nowadays, on weekends, my mother teaches me how to cook. You know, I learnt to make dhoklas this weekend.'

Just when Hitesh decided he couldn't carry on any longer and should take her leave, she broke in, 'Is it okay for me to work after marriage?'

Hitesh was startled. He hesitated and said, 'I think it's okay for any girl to work and have a career. It's for two people to decide.'

'Oh, that's great! You're very modern,' she said admiringly, nodding her head. Her pink mobile phone rang to the tune of the latest Bollywood number, and she quickly turned it off.

Hitesh was suddenly annoyed at his mother for dragging him into this. He missed Sandra. 'Okay, listen. I need to leave for a meeting in five minutes. I am calling for the bill,' he said.

'But I wanted to order gulab jamun,' she said, making a small face again.

'Ask them to parcel it for you. Sorry, I have to go.' They got up soon after and walked out together. She looked crestfallen and her face wore an annoyed expression.

'You didn't tell me how I look,' she said icily.

'Nice. Very nice,' Hitesh said hurriedly, taking out his shades and putting them on. 'Hope to see you again.'

'Yes,' she said with a faint smile and walked towards a rickshaw that stood outside the shopping centre.

Hitesh started his bike and sped away.

■

He reached office a little before two, and walked in to find Sandra glued to the computer screen. 'Mr Mehta was looking for you. He said that Mr Reddy wants to see you, and discuss the progress of the audit assignment,' she spoke tersely. The old Mehta had been briefed by many about Hitesh's findings. He had realized that a lot of the information came as news to him, and he was anxious about the precarious situation the company was in.

'Okay, I'll go. Did you have lunch?' he asked, picking up his notepad and file.

'Yes, I did. How was yours with that tart?'

'Who? What?'

'Don't pretend! The girl your mother wants you to marry. You had saved her picture on the desktop. Seems some docile girl of the '80s! Good for you. When is the wedding?' she said nonchalantly.

'There's no wedding. Let me explain…'

'No, thank you. Please go on with your meeting. I have a lot of work to finish.'

Hitesh felt despondent but was pressed for time to speak further, though he was secretly delighted to see Sandra jealous of the other women in his life. He thought he would take her out for dinner in the evening and explain. He felt elated at the plan and walked towards Mehta's cabin.

■

Hitesh entered the cabin slowly. Mehta greeted him with enthusiasm and patted him on his back. 'Burning the midnight oil, eh, young man?' he said.

'Yes, it has been hectic. We are slated to wrap up in two days.'

'Hmm… See, Mr Reddy is very worried. I've briefed him about many of your findings. He wants to meet and discuss things with you, in person. He has kept his afternoon free for you. You should go to him now. Just confirm with his secretary, Payal, before you enter.'

'I'll do that,' Hitesh said and walked out. He reached the top floor of the building and, getting out of the elevator, walked towards a large mahogany desk. A pleasant and busy-looking girl, wearing a pair of thick glasses and hair tied in a knot, sat behind the desk.

'Payal?' he asked.

'Yes. Are you Mr Hitesh from Smith & Donald?'

Hitesh nodded.

'Please go in. Sir is expecting you,' she said politely and resumed typing on the keyboard.

'Thank you,' he said with a smile and walked towards a large door. It opened to a room five times the size of Mehta's cabin. There was a large desk with a monitor and a laptop at one end of the room. The other end had a round table surrounded by chairs on one side, and a plush sofa set on the other. Huge paintings adorned the walls. A glass cabinet neatly decorated with trophies and certificates graced another corner.

'Ah, Hitesh,' he heard his name called out in a thick South Indian accent. A tall, dark and plump man walked in from a room connected to the office from the inside. 'I was resting after lunch,' he said. Hitesh noticed the stylish suit the man wore, his Rolex watch and gold cufflinks, and felt a little intimidated.

'Let's sit and chat,' he said, walking towards the sofa set. His huge frame seemed to carry off his designer suit quite well.

'What will you drink?' the man asked with a friendly smile.

'A glass of water will be good,' Hitesh said, overwhelmed by his presence. As if on cue, Payal walked in.

'Bring me a bottle of Cabernet Shiraz and two glasses, please,' he said with warmth. Hitesh wanted to stop him, but couldn't.

'So, I've heard about the problems in the company. The situation is grave and it's difficult for me to face the board. I wonder what can be done.' Hitesh realized that Reddy had little control over the company's affairs; the plant was run by a bunch of crooks, while Mehta managed Finances and the firm's appearances to outsiders.

'Yes, it is a precarious situation, Mr Reddy. The report from our side will highlight the on-going issue of concern,' Hitesh said mechanically, to which Mr Reddy froze and glared at him angrily. He calmed down almost immediately and cleared his throat. Payal walked in with a bottle of wine and glasses. She poured some into each glass, placed them on the glass table before them and walked out, without saying a word, almost like she was invisible. 'Cheers,' Reddy said, raising his glass, and egging on Hitesh to take his.

'Look, since you've worked with everyone at the plant, I need your advice. If you were in my shoes, what would you do?' On seeing Hitesh hesitate, he added, 'I'm meeting you and asking you as a friend.' He smiled broadly and leaned back, seemingly enjoying his drink while Hitesh made a funny face after a sip from his glass. 'I need this company to continue with business, at any cost; at least for a while. If it doesn't, it would be difficult for me...Very difficult!' Hitesh looked uneasy and wondered what to say. It was beyond his brief and professional duty to advise the head of a large conglomerate.

'I would send out a message to these people. A clear, stern message that things won't go the way they have been anymore,' Hitesh began.

'Go on,' Reddy said, looking at him with interest.

'I would fire R.V. Suresh, who controls purchasing—a big portion of the budget—and is making a killing. You have the papers; over hundred crores in five years.'

'What about Vinod and Varun?'

'Vinod controls Human Resources. He is crafty and can rally people around him, as he's been more of a representative of the workers, than of the company.'

'Yes, true...' Reddy said and continued to stare at Hitesh.

'But I would send someone in from Finance, and de-link the housing department from him. That's where he makes his money: make Finance take over payroll functions, and the running of the housing department. It will stem the flow.'

'Exactly!' Reddy burst out with childlike glee.

'With Varun, you have to use another tactic.' Hitesh was now in his element. 'You need him; he's in-charge of sales, and is extremely well-connected. He manages a network of dealers, does the paperwork and moves a fleet of vehicles across the country. You need to work on him, by threat or otherwise, to highlight the corruption and sleaze that he's been a part of.'

'Hmm... Let's see how I can manage that. Maybe we'll straighten him out and keep him on for a while.'

'Mohan Babu, a dangerous man, is connected with a lot of ground support. He can make a lot of noise and stifle progress. He has to be brought in line, either by threat or through any other means.'

Reddy looked defiant and outraged. 'I agree; he's a troublemaker.'

'You might want to make use of the rumour that he got the executive, who stood up to him, murdered.'

'Is it? Clever!' he said in a contemplative mood, and scratched his chin. 'It's time for some decisive action and you've given us some strong evidence that we can use.'

'More importantly, Mr Reddy, you need fresh ideas for the company. Your models are outdated, and the customer needs and expectations have changed.'

'Yes, it's a dead company, to be honest...'

'All might not be lost. Look at Axis Car rental, the largest car rental service in the world. It began when Kansas Motors was in trouble; the entire fleet is made up of their cars,' Hitesh grinned with his recently acquired knowledge.

'What are you saying?' Reddy was surprised.

'You can do the same, Mr Reddy. India is developing. There are many tier-two cities that could use such a service, where the big agencies aren't active yet. You are manufacturing cars that have no real consumer appeal anyway.'

Reddy looked relieved. 'You are a creative accountant, I must say. What ideas! Let me think about this.' Reddy was clearly impressed.

Hitesh smiled and took a sip from his glass. It still tasted strong and bitter, but he braced a smile and took another.

'Why don't you come over this evening for the music release party of my upcoming film? It's at the Taj Banjara.'

Hitesh was both surprised and elated. He had never before been invited to a high-end party. But he was apprehensive and thus hesitated. 'Actually, Mr Reddy, I need to finish a lot of...'

'I would like you to meet a few people tonight. Many celebrities will be there too. You'll enjoy yourself. Payal will give you an invitation and discuss other details. I have an important engagement to attend to, so if you'll excuse me,' he said, standing up and shaking Hitesh's hand with force.

Hitesh staggered out, dazed by the opulence in Reddy's office. He stood before Payal, who was on the phone, helping someone with directions to reach the office.

'Do you have a tuxedo?' she asked after she had hung up.

'No.'

'Well, go out and get one this evening. You might find a good deal at Raymond's. The party starts at eight. Here's the invite. You can bring someone along with you, your wife or a girlfriend, like a date,' she said, with a practised smile.

'Sure. Yes, I understand,' he said, intimidated by the idea of buying a new suit for the party.

'Are you coming as well?' he asked.

'No, I don't go to these parties. Not my scene, really,' she said, emphasizing the last few words.

'Black would be the best,' she said gingerly, before she reached to answer a call.

'Mr Reddy's office,' she said in a rehearsed, professional tone as Hitesh turned around, and walked back to the meeting room, their makeshift office.

■

Many thoughts muddled Hitesh's mind. Would he face trouble from Mohan Babu and other crooks, now that he had disclosed their scams to Venugopal Reddy? What would Sahil say? But more than anything, he needed to clarify things with Sandra. He had begun to like her, despite her work-shirking ways. He had made up his mind to attend the party, with Sandra as his partner. She would be thrilled, he thought.

He walked in to see Sandra typing away furiously. 'Mr Reddy has invited me to a party he's hosting tonight. Do you want to come?'

She shook her head and continued with her work.

'I'm not interested in that girl; she's not my type. My mother forced me into that situation. It was painful to even sit there, listening to her ramblings. What could I do?'

Sandra didn't respond. She got up and went towards the printer. She handed him her working papers and, in a tone of irritation, said, 'Could you review these please? I've been working late everyday. I need to leave on time today.'

'You're still angry with me. Come on. Let's go to this party tonight. The client wants us to come.' Hitesh was surprised at his own enthusiasm, and realized that he too craved for the high life like most others.

'Wants you to come,' Sandra corrected him. 'You please go there. Take your relative along with you; she seems to be much fun.'

'Relax, will you?' he said, taking her hand in his, which she withdrew immediately.

'Don't touch me!' she screamed. 'Just review my work, and let me leave.'

'Sorry,' Hitesh said. 'Don't worry about getting late; I'll drop you home. Let's go and eat something in the canteen. We can work after that.' Sandra shook her head and continued to work, while Hitesh got up to get a bottle of water from the pantry.

He was walking through a corridor just when he heard Sandra talking on phone in whispers with someone. He stopped. He heard her throwing kisses over the phone and giggling. Hitesh confronted her. She went pale. 'I'll talk to you later,' she softly said and hung up. Hitesh stood quietly for a moment and turned to walk away when she stopped him. 'It was my boyfriend. We have made up,' she said and bit her lower lip. Hitesh's face wore an angry expression. 'You aren't going to complain about me, are you? Er, I have been doing all my work.' Hitesh recoiled at hearing that, and turned to focus on the working papers lying next to him.

CHAPTER 5

Hitesh entered home carrying four shopping bags, noticing the surprise on his father's face, who sat in front of the television, reclining completely, feet on the table, wearing a vest and pajamas.

'Got promotion kya?' he asked with sarcasm. His mother walked into the living room looking furious.

'No, I have to attend a party hosted by a client, Mr Venugopal Reddy.'

'Who? That film producer?'

'Yes. His family also owns Supreme Motors.'

'I know, I know. A high-society ruffian; he has many political links; very sleazy reputation. Not good,' his father shook his head dismissively.

'Okay, Papa. Now I need to get ready and leave. It isn't like he is my best friend. We have to do these things for client relationships.'

'Ask him for a job. He will pay you more than the bloodsuckers.'

'Do you realize what you have done today?' his mother began.

'What happened, Ma?'

'Arey, look at this fellow; pretending as if nothing has happened! You were rude to poor Dimple, were you not? I had to call your Mama and apologize. He said sorry to her father. She has been crying all day. She says that you didn't talk to her. What did you do! She is such a good girl. Decent, working...'

'Ma, I'm not in a mood for this, really. I have to go,' he said in a tone of finality and walked over to his room for a shower. He reappeared in the hall a few minutes later. 'I'm not going to marry her. Never!' he said firmly before putting on his pair of new shoes, and walking out of the house.

An hour later, he was at the ballroom in Taj Banjara, bang on time. The party was yet to begin, with only a few hangers-on, caterers and hotel staff around.

He lurked around by the pool outside. He thought about Sandra and felt terrible. He thought about his job and felt worse. Even home was no respite, with his mother forever looking for girls for him and his father disapproving of every career move he made.

Someone tapped on his shoulder. Hitesh turned around to see a beautiful girl standing before him. She was dressed in formal attire, hair neatly tied in a knot.

'Sushma Ragavhan! What a surprise!'

'Hitesh Patel! I saw you walking towards the pool, and took a break to come here,' she said, flashing her beautiful smile. 'You have changed quite a lot, I must say! Looking good.'

'Thank you,' he grinned. 'I'm here for Venugopal Reddy's party. He's one of our clients.'

'Ah, Venu Reddy, the hot-shot producer! Very nice. Look at you; you've made it big in life. What do you do exactly?'

'I'm a manager at Smith & Donald,' he lied. 'I manage a number of MNC clients, a very busy job. It's one of the world's largest accounting and audit firms.'

She looked at him with a glimmer in her eyes. Hitesh felt ecstatic as the realization dawned upon him; he had impressed the most popular girl from his junior college days, someone he had spoken to only twice in two years. She still had a shapely figure and a regal air about her. Her beautiful tresses had brown highlights and he noticed the kohl in her eyes.

'So, a nice six-figure salary, huh?' she asked, interrupting his thoughts. He felt utterly embarrassed, but managed a smile and shook his head politely.

'It's a very stressful life; meetings and travelling all the time. A lot of pressure,' he said, sounding rushed. 'What about you? You used to model back in college.'

'Yes, I did a few print ads back then. Wanted to try the ramp, but I am a little short for it. I studied hotel management, and came here,' she answered, then hesitated a little and added, 'I tried my luck at acting, knocked on many doors, went to many auditions. But it didn't quite work out. There are thousands like me—strugglers.' She looked jaded, and he could sense the frustration in her voice.

'Life isn't easy,' he consoled.

'Do you have a smoke?' she asked.

'No, I'm afraid not. I don't smoke.'

'Some things haven't changed. Do you want to go out and get one? Give me company; your party won't start before ten.'

'Sure,' he said, following her out into the garden and towards the back gate of the hotel. He walked over to the little kiosk and picked up a pack of Classic Milds for her.

'So, have you been living in Hyderabad itself?' he asked with interest, as she lit her cigarette.

'No, I moved back here three months ago. It's not bad, rather good to come back home. I spent five difficult years in Mumbai; didn't get anywhere with anything. I got an opportunity in Hyderabad, so here I am. I'm twenty-seven anyway; a little old to be doing films.'

'Hmm...You shouldn't give up. Who knows, something good may come up?'

'Well, not hoping for it makes life easier. So, tell me about you. Are you married?'

'No.'

'Girlfriend?'

'Not anymore,' he lied again.

'Aw, you look quite heartbroken. Who was she?'

'A girl who works in my team...' Hitesh replied, and wished she wouldn't ask more.

'Oh, love in the office! Nice. And what happened?'

'She went back to her ex-boyfriend,' he said, and immediately regretted it.

'Darn! Relationships today are damn complicated. I broke up before I moved here too. My boyfriend was a yoga instructor.'

Hitesh somehow felt good to hear that. Was he attracted to her? He wondered why Sushma was taking interest in him. He gazed at her with curiosity, reflecting on the past few days. The sleaze and corruption at Supreme Motors, his fling with Sandra, Venu Reddy's hand of friendship and now Sushma's interest in him.

'I have to get back now. I am on duty till late tonight. I finish at two. Maybe if you get done with the party, and I finish off with my duty, we can catch up again,' she said all of a sudden.

'Yes. That will be great, Sushma!'

'Sush,' she said with a smile. 'Friends call me Sush.'

He walked back to the party, following her lead, his eyes fixed on her curvy frame as she gracefully walked towards the hotel entrance.

They exchanged numbers before she retired to her desk, and then he headed towards the ballroom. As he entered, he noticed the large crowd that had gathered there. He walked right in, a bit hesitant, looking for a familiar face.

Mehta waved to him. He happily moved across the room to greet him and his family, and spent the next hour talking to him about the problems at the plant, the general business environment and politics. An array of starters and drinks kept doing the rounds.

At around 11 p.m., Venugopal Reddy, along with the cast and crew, unveiled the music CDs of his upcoming film, with the Education Minister G.S. Rao in tow.

A few moments later, while Hitesh was having dinner, Venugopal walked up to him. 'Glad to see you here. Hope you're enjoying the party,' he beamed.

'Yes, Mr Reddy, thanks. It's been quite a nice experience. I've never been to such a party before,' he said, looking over his shoulder at the swarm of media people present at the event. He noticed that there were more photographers, cameramen and journalists than the invitees.

'Come, I want you to meet the minister. I've been discussing with people about your idea of a car rental company; I think it's a sound one. It could help us save Supreme Motors.'

'I think it would,' Hitesh said weakly. It struck him that he hadn't really thought about this idea after his last meeting with Reddy; he had been more occupied with the new sweet-and-sour experiences he had had with women in the past couple of weeks.

'The minister is a good friend of mine, and he is keen to invest in the new business idea,' Venugopal said softly, his breath reeking of whisky and eyes bloodshot.

The Minister G.S. Rao stood with his supporters and security guards, conversing with the cast and crew of the film. They gave way on seeing Venugopal approaching him. Minister Rao, noticing him, came forward with a smile.

'A wonderful event!' he said in a thick South Indian accent. He smiled after each word, keeping a humble disposition, conscious of the reporters lingering around.

'This is Hitesh Patel, the young accountant I talked to you about,' Venugopal introduced him to the minister, one arm on his shoulder. Minister Rao joined his palms, head inclined to one side, and showed his paan-stained, crooked teeth. Hitesh cringed.

'Very good ideas, sir! Today's young people are the future,' he said blankly. Hitesh noticed Mehta standing quietly a few metres behind them.

'Thank you, sir,' Hitesh said meekly.

'You should implement your ideas. We will support you,' the minister said. He watched Hitesh carefully from the corner of his eye, assessing his every word and gesture.

'Thanks for coming to the event, Rao Garu. I will speak to you before you leave,' Venugopal smiled, signaling that the introduction was over.

'It was wonderful meeting you, sir,' Hitesh said, as G.S. Rao smiled politely in response and moved away.

Venugopal turned towards Hitesh. 'You need to think more about this idea of yours. Let us meet for breakfast at the Sheraton on Monday morning. We can discuss how we can develop this further,' he said as he walked towards the exit with Hitesh following him.

'But Mr Reddy, the audit...I'm not sure what role...'

'This has nothing to do with the audit. Let's sit and talk on Monday morning. This might just prove to be very beneficial for you, and your career.'

Hitesh looked up at him with a confused smile, wondering what was in store for him this Monday.

'I'll see you on Monday morning at the Sheraton,' he said, before walking out of the party, and towards the front desk at the hotel. He noticed that Sushma was pleased to see him.

'Had fun at the launch?' she asked.

'Oh, I did. It was good, for sure. Are you done for the day?'

'Yeah...'

'How do you get home?'

'Normally the hotel driver drops us but...I can ride back with you.'

'Sure, let's go,' he said beaming with enthusiasm.

She picked up her bag and walked out of the lobby, a couple of steps behind Hitesh. After a short bike ride in Banjara Hills, he dropped her off at her apartment in Begumpet.

'That was a nice ride! What are you doing tomorrow?' she asked while getting off his bike.

'I may sleep in a bit, but I'm likely to be summoned to office for a review.'

'It's Sunday! Well, listen. I am on duty during the day, but why don't you pick me up at four? We can go watch a film, and maybe have dinner together.'

'Sure. Good idea,' he answered, trying to contain his excitement.

'Bye then,' she said in her sweet voice. He removed his helmet. Sushma stepped forward and kissed him on the cheek while playfully ruffling his hair.

'Goodnight!' he gushed, before starting his bike. He dreamed about her all through the way back home. He couldn't believe his luck! Was Sushma walking into his life? His mind told him not to jump to conclusions, and be patient. But Hitesh knew that whatever it turned out to be with Sushma, she had come as a breeze of fresh air in his life.

CHAPTER 6

Hitesh waited anxiously at the coffee shop in the lobby of ITC Sheraton. He glanced worriedly at the menu; the price of a cup of tea was over hundred rupees, and that of a sandwich, over two hundred. He waved away the young uniformed lady who stood before him with a plastic smile, saying that he was waiting for someone.

Sahil's name flashed on his phone. *Oh God, not now,* he thought. He ignored the call, and went back to browsing through the menu. It listed items he had never heard of before, and he couldn't even pronounce some of the names.

Venugopal Reddy walked in minutes later, with an air of authority in his gait, as he headed towards the table where Hitesh was sitting.

'Hope you haven't been waiting for too long,' he said, before shaking Hitesh's hand and settling into the comfy sofa chair.

'Rashmi, please get me a cheese sandwich, a latte and a bottle of Evian. Thanks. What about you, Hitesh? Tea or coffee? Something to eat?'

'Thank you. I'll have an espresso please,' Hitesh said, shifting uneasily in his chair. The waitress smiled at him. He had ordered the cheapest item listed in the beverages section.

'That's a black coffee, sir. Are you okay with that?'

'No, no. Please put some milk,' Hitesh said.

'Will that be a cappuccino instead, sir?' She smiled broadly, while Venugopal punched away at the keys on his smartphone.

'Yes, yes. That's okay.' The lady went away, and Hitesh heaved a sigh of relief.

'So Hitesh, this idea of yours... Tell me, how will this car rental company work?'

'The company should be set up as a 24x7 cab service, a separate entity from Supreme Motors. You should ideally set this up in fifteen to twenty B-towns, where new airports have come up, and cities experiencing rapid growth.'

'Hmm...what about the investment? How do we make money in this venture?'

'What the company should do is: buy the fleet from Supreme Motors at a twenty per cent discount, specially manufactured with CNG-fitted kits, and give these cars on a long term lease at full cost to franchisees in each city. They'll operate in their territories on agreed terms.'

'Franchisees?'

'Yes. In each city you bring on board a franchisee that would invest in leasing a fleet of fifty cars, and have exclusive rights to operate in the name of the brand in that city. In turn, they'll pay twenty-five per cent of the takings to the cab company. This will help cover centralized billing and customer service and marketing, and help return a healthy profit. On top of that, the company would take fifty per cent of any branding or advertising on, or in the vehicles.'

'That's a fantastic idea! But do you think we'd be able to get enough number of investors, to come on board as franchisees?'

'I think you would. There's a lot of money out there. I'm sure the money can be found. A recent study by *Business Forever* shows a 180 per cent increase in investment in franchise businesses. There are forums and conclaves held to convince investors about the business model. I've done an analysis on returns considering fuel economy, maintenance costs and other expenses; nearly fifty per cent of the total fare would go as expenses on fuel and maintenance; drivers work on a commission of fifteen per cent and the franchise owner keeps a good ten per cent.'

'Hmm…' Venugopal looked at Hitesh with appreciation.

'A man like Varun, who heads sales now, could easily attract, build and manage a network of franchisees. He's been managing dealerships everywhere. He needs to be managed carefully though.'

'How about you coming on board and running this new company? You're a finance man,' Venugopal beamed at him, while observing him from the corner of his eye. 'The minister, G.S. Rao, who is a close associate, will co-invest with me in this venture. We want a trustworthy and capable person.'

Hitesh hadn't expected this in his wildest dreams. 'Me, sir? I don't have any experience in running a company…I'm an auditor.'

'It's your idea; only you could know how to execute it best,' Venugopal leaned in before picking up his cup of coffee and taking a sip. 'What do you make now?'

Hitesh hesitated. 'Roughly thirty-five thousand in-hand, sir, after tax deductions.'

'You get paid peanuts! We'll pay you five times as much. Most of this will be off the books, paid to an account off-shore. You bring on a team of four to five people; take Varun as well, and start this thing.

'We'll look after you,' he said in a persuasive tone and added, 'you'll be the CEO.'

The words rang in Hitesh's ears, and almost made him spring out of his comfortable chair. 'I'll think about it. Thanks for your offer, sir, it's very kind of you,' Hitesh said, trying hard to control his excitement.

'Thank you. You're a very capable boy. You are most suitable to kick-start this venture.'

'I will think about it, sir, and get back to you tomorrow.'

'Sure. And I wanted to talk to you about this audit. Can you tone things down a notch? There are many issues of concern in your findings, and these will be resolved once the new company is in place.'

'Hmm... Yes, the company has its problems, but I'll see what I can do. At the end of the day, it's my boss at the firm who will review my report. But you're right. The cab service should turn things around, albeit very quickly.'

'Thanks, Hitesh! Please soften up the findings. I am relying on you; I'll wait for your call. Let's wrap up, I have a meeting in a short while.'

'Yes, sir,' Hitesh said, wondering what he could do about the damned findings.

■

Hitesh walked out with a broad grin on his face, feeling as if he was walking on the clouds. His phone buzzed again; this time he picked it up. 'Hello, Sahil.'

'Haan, sir. Busy man! You didn't take my call earlier,' Sahil said, sarcasm obvious in his tone.

'I was in a meeting with Mr Reddy,' Hitesh retorted.

'So, what is the progress? I dropped into office yesterday, and didn't see you. You're normally around...'

'Yesterday was Sunday. It's a holiday.'

'Yaar, I want to review the work. Wrap it up today and come to office with the files tonight.'

'It's just not possible, sir; we won't be able to wrap it up till the end of this week. There is a lot of work and documentation underway. You can review it next Monday.'

Sahil noticed a new assertiveness in Hitesh's voice, which infuriated him. 'Yaar, what is this attitude? You have failed to meet your deadline! Seems like you're no longer interested in a promotion; come to my office after work. I want to meet you.'

'Sahil, I can no longer do this. If you want me to come to office after a long day at work, I'll be there. But I'll bring my resignation with me because I'm tired of this,' Hitesh said with a raised pitch.

'Arey yaar, relax! I just want to meet you and see if there are any difficulties. Why are you getting upset? We'll review the file on Monday. I'll tell Boss that the client is delaying the work.' His tone changed from accusing to pleading. 'You're among the best people I have.'

'Alright. I need to go for a meeting now. Please don't put unnecessary pressure on me; I have a life too,' Hitesh said in a firm voice.

'I understand; calm down!' Sahil added, before hanging up. Hitesh felt good about himself. The approach that Sushma suggested he adopt, over dinner last night, had worked. She had stopped him from going to office on an off-day, and the two of them had watched a movie instead.

He received a text message from Sandra before he got on his bike. 'Hitesh, I'm leaving for home. My grandfather is very sick. I don't think I can come to the office tomorrow. Thanks.'

'Bloody hell! Another late night. Even the dinner with Sushma might not be possible,' Hitesh muttered under his breath.

Two hours later, as he was poring over the working papers, Mehta knocked on the glass outside Hitesh's cabin. He stood up and opened the door, letting the elderly gentleman in.

'So, how was the meeting with Venu this morning?' he asked with a knowing smile.

'It went quite well. We had a fruitful discussion,' Hitesh said, maintaining a professional tone.

'Good. I hope it works out. He mentioned that you would go easy on us, considering the company now has robust plans for the future,' he added with a smirk.

'I guess. The findings still are subject to review,' he replied with some hesitance.

'So the girl has run off again, huh? You seem to be knee deep with work, as usual.'

'Her grandfather is unwell…'

'Really? I saw her getting into a car and leaving with a young man. She seemed to be in high spirits. I was parking my car; she didn't notice me, of course.' He wore a contemptuous grin, and set his gaze on the scattered documents on Hitesh's table.

'The assignment hasn't been managed to our expectation,' Mehta sighed, 'but you're one of our own now. We'll support you,' he continued, while Hitesh looked uneasy, like he had been boxed into a corner.

He resumed with his work after Mehta left, and spent the next couple of hours refining his work papers and generously toning down some of his findings. *It's time for me to move on from this thankless job,* he thought, annoyed.

He called up Sushma, who picked up her phone on the first ring. 'Coffee tonight, Sush?'

'Hmm…I get done at two.'

'Sure. I'll be working till around that time too; I'll come pick you up.'

'For coffee?'

'Yeah, the café at Sheraton should be open; they serve nice cappuccino.'

'Ah, interesting! Can't wait to see you,' she chirped before hanging up.

CHAPTER 7

Sahil and Hitesh were concluding their final, hour-long audit review meeting with Venugopal Reddy and Mehta, who appeared ill at ease with questions pointed towards them by Sahil.

'Rest assured, Sahil, the company is on a path of recovery. We are concluding some important trade deals. Our car will be marketed more for the trade, as opposed to focusing on individual needs of customers,' Venugopal said in a rehearsed tone. 'We have cut costs too...'

'This might be true, but, as per the books, your owing is deeply worrying, considering that sales are stagnant and the cash position is precarious,' Sahil said while flipping pages of a report that Hitesh had prepared.

'It may be that some of these amounts have been renegotiated or written off, as per the notes I've made,' Hitesh said, coming to the rescue of a worried Venugopal.

'We are restructuring everything; you will see the results soon. On your way out, you will notice a few gentlemen waiting in the lobby; they are the managers at the manufacturing facility. Some will be let go today, and the roles of some others will be reassigned. We are infusing new blood into the business, and Hitesh has done a great job pointing out some of our weaknesses,' Venugopal said forcefully and smiled in Hitesh's direction, who winced at the mention of his name.

'So, Hitesh, are you of the opinion that an issue of concern does not arise?' Sahil said, looking at Hitesh.

'Probably not at this point, but it needs to be reevaluated next year. We've made a few points on efficiencies related to production, purchases and sales, which the board must take note of. These have been included in our report addressed to them.'

'So, Mr Reddy, I think we've been cooperative and understanding in our approach with your management. Will we be confirmed as auditors for the next year as well? In which case, we would be looking at a fee hike, given our efforts,' Sahil said, smiling from Venugopal to Mehta.

'We will make a proposal to the board to retain you as auditors for the next year,' Venugopal nodded. 'Mr Mehta, please note a fifteen per cent fee increase, which we should consider, and approve of in our meeting.'

'Yes, Mr Reddy,' Mehta said, before scratching numbers in his diary, nodding along.

'Wonderful. We hope the new plans bear fruit, Mr Reddy. We'll see you soon. Hitesh will be in touch with you, as soon as the partner signs on the Audit Report,' Sahil said, before standing up and adjusting his new suit. Hitesh eyed his designer tie with envy.

'Thank you. It was wonderful working with Hitesh; he's a great talent,' Venugopal said, patting his back, while Sahil stretched his lips into a broad smile.

Hitesh walked out and, on his way, noticed Varun Rao, G.V. Vinod, Mohan Babu and R.V. Suresh sitting in the lobby outside Venugopal's office. They turned to look at him angrily when he wished them good morning. Mohan Babu almost growled at him, noticing which he quietly crept away behind Sahil.

'Ha ha, those morons are in the soup! They look like they want to kill you, huh? Bach ke reh,' Sahil snickered in the elevator.

'Yes, one or two of them might get fired...'

'Sounds fun; so, you seem to have made a very good impression on them, huh? Acha hai. The MD was praising you profusely,' Sahil said.

■

Moments later, R.V. Suresh was summoned to Venugopal's cabin by Payal, while Mohan Babu sat outside, dressed in a cheap suit, a defiant smile on the face, gaping at her lecherously.

R.V. Suresh walked in with a nervous smile, and stood prostrate in front of Venugopal, who sat back with a grim expression and stared at him coldly. Mehta kept his eyes fixed upon a bundle of papers before him.

'So, how are things at the factory?' Venugopal asked, feigning interest.

'With God's grace, everything is good, sir.'

'Do you know why you're here?'

'No, sir. Tell me, sir. Anything I can help with?'

'Hmm… We've been going through a lot of documents, and some irregularities we've come across are startling. Do you know we pay around thirty per cent more on components than our peers?'

'We do careful evaluation always, sir. We have a tendering process…'

'We have only six firms doing bulk of the supply and, strangely, these firms don't supply to any other auto major,' Reddy said, with raised eyebrows.

'Sir…'

'And all these firms are owned by you, directly or indirectly.'

'Sir, let me explain…' R.V. Suresh pleaded. Mehta nodded his head in dismay.

'You don't have to explain; we have a full understanding of what's going on. You're fired!'

'I have been in this company for fifteen years, sir.'

'You're fired and my decision is final! As per the books, these firms are owed two crore rupees. We will pay nothing and the amount will be written off. Is that right?'

'I will be destroyed, sir, I have borrowed to buy…'

'Leave. Get out of my office, now!' Reddy screamed in rage. Mehta refused to look up.

A defeated Suresh, despondence written on his face, slowly walked out of the cabin, and shut the door behind him.

Soon after, G.V. Vinod walked in. He looked baffled, and sat opposite Venugopal.

'I have just fired Suresh on account of fraud and misrepresentation,' Venugopal began in a high-pitched voice. Vinod averted his gaze, and felt a lump rising up in his throat.

'Yes, sir…'

'Complete his paperwork, and settle his PF and gratuity. I don't want to see that man set his foot in the company premises ever again.'

'As you say, sir…'

'While you're here, Vinod, there's a thing or two that I need to discuss with you; things that trouble me…'

'Tell me, sir,' Vinod said meekly.

'I hear that there are some employees on the rolls, people who don't work for the company, but get paid a salary by us every month.'

'I'm not sure, sir. I'll have to check up…'

'There are fifty such cases, Vinod. Our auditor has given us a full report,' Mehta said softly, looking sympathetic, while Venugopal looked outraged.

'I'll have this fixed, sir. Please give me two to three months. I'll clean up everything…'

'You have until the end of this month,' Venugopal said, taking a puff from his cigarette, and blowing off the smoke in Vinod's direction.

'Yes, sir.'

'Then there is this other matter; I've heard about a lot of irregularities in the housing complex. It has come to my notice that people are running businesses from there: there's a catering service, a lawyer's office…There was also a rumour of a brothel. What is going on, Vinod?'

'My enemies are spreading rumours, sir. I always work in the interest of the company and the workers.'

'Mr Mehta is allocating an executive from his department, to run the housing department. You will hand over everything to him, and focus simply on Human Resources.' Vinod, stung on hearing this, looked up at Mehta, who wore a relaxed smile.

'Yes, sir; I'll do as you instruct me.'

'That's what I wanted to hear; I sense that people's loyalties in our company lie elsewhere.'

'No, sir...' Vinod protested weakly.

'And another important matter; please transfer the last one year's rent to the company's account, by the end of this week.'

'Sir?'

'The rent that the illegal occupants have been paying you; I seem to have some receipts here that are being given out by G.V. Housing Services whose total estimate is about fifty lakhs. I expect the full amount to be transferred to the company's account by the end of this week,' he said, flaring his nostrils, and pointing his finger in Vinod's direction.

'Please give me till the end of the month, sir,' he pleaded.

'Two weeks, not a day more. And I expect to see full loyalty from you, Vinod. The things that I have heard, and the evidence that I have seen, make me doubtful of your loyalty towards the company.'

'Yes, sir. I'm servant of the company, sir,' he said, before folding his palms, and falling at Venugopal's feet.

'Leave,' Venugopal spat at him, unaffected by the gesture.

'Transfer him to the head office in six months, and retire him at the end of the year,' Venugopal said to Mehta, who diligently made a note.

Mohan Babu and Varun Rao were kept waiting while Venugopal took a break for lunch and a short siesta in his room behind the cabin. Payal sent Varun Rao in at 3 p.m.

'Come, Varun. Sit down. Tell me what's happening on the sales front; we seem to be manufacturing a lot of cars and selling very few.'

'The market is difficult, sir. Tastes and preferences have changed but we are doing well, sir.'

'Is it?' Venugopal growled fixing his steady gaze at him.

'Yes, not so bad, sir,' Varun said, this time less convincingly, as Venugopal sat back with a stony expression that remained unchanged for a few minutes.

'Anyway, I think you've spent a lot of time selling cars,' Venugopal finally said and paused, and lit up again.

'Yes, sir. I've been here for eight long years…'

'I'd like you move to another venture that I am promoting.'

'I don't know much about the film industry, sir,' he said, looking confused.

'No, this is a cab service. It will be among the biggest in the country; a legitimate, powerful venture, unlike the loss-making manufacturing set up we run.'

'That's wonderful! Where do you see me adding value to the project, sir?' Varun Rao's eyes lit up.

'I want you to come on board as the operational head. The company will operate through franchisees in various cities. You'll have to set up and manage the franchisee network, and bring forth people who want to come on board as franchisees.'

'Yes, I can do that. I have contacts with dealers and people in the transport business. No problem, sir. I'll move whenever you tell me.'

'Very good! I like you, Varun. That's why I've decided to forgive your minor indiscretions,' Venugopal said with a knowing smile.

'Sir?'

'I'm well aware of what you've been up to; conniving with the production guys and then selling cars with minor defects at a major profit. I keep my ears and eyes open, Varun.'

'I'm sorry, sir. This will never happen again.' Varun's face had turned white.

'I believe you. Now it will be kind of you to remit the profits made through this side venture to the company; the profits from the last three years, if you will.'

'It will be done, sir,' Varun said, gritting his teeth.

'Good, I hope your loyalties don't waver in the future. Get ready to move to Hyderabad. Say goodbye to your old friends,' Venugopal said, standing up to shake his hand and indicating that the meeting was over.

Mohan Babu was called in an hour later. He was made to sit outside all day, watching his colleagues walk in and out, with varied expressions on their faces. Suresh had looked horrified, Vinod had appeared relieved, though a bit troubled, and Varun Rao had walked out with a smug grin.

He sat opposite Venugopal with a defiant look on his face, and looked him straight in the eye.

'Mohan Babu,' Venugopal smiled. 'You were supposed to be my trusted lieutenant.'

'I am a servant of the company, saar.'

'That's not the impression your friends and colleagues give me,' Venugopal rebuked sharply.

'Why? What have I done?'

'You have been running all kinds of scams: from setting up shell companies to supply components, fake employee accounts that do not exist, letting out company property for personal gain, running a whore house from the housing complex... Should I continue? The list is endless.' Mehta shook his head and excused himself from the cabin.

'Who spread that last rumour? All lies! I am not responsible for any of this,' he screamed. His blood pressure shot up and he looked aghast.

'I have all the evidence, and it has been confirmed in my meetings with your other colleagues this morning,' Venugopal said calmly, shifting his gaze from Mohan Babu, to the file lying open before him.

'Saar, I will tell you. I am not responsible. I am an ordinary...'

The door opened and G.S. Rao, the minister, walked in, wearing his trademark starch white kurta and dhoti. Mohan Babu leapt up from his seat and prostrated before him while Rao ignored him, and moved ahead to shake hands with Venugopal Reddy. After some small talk, they sat down, Rao fiddling with the buttons on his kurta.

'What Babu, I'm hearing many complaints against you. What is all this?' Rao chastened Mohan Babu, who turned his gaze away to the rug.

'To this is the added allegation of the murder of an executive; complaints against you don't seem to end. Just the other day a journalist called me up,' Venugopal said, turning to G.S. Rao, who closed his eyes and shook his head.

'Political career finished,' G.S. Rao declared.

'No saar, I swear. I have done nothing, saar. I will do whatever you ask me to do,' Mohan Babu pleaded.

'Babu has worked quite hard for the workers' rights; such a promising labour leader, alas!' Venugopal sighed. 'I will have to call the police in this case. Fraud, murder...'

'Venugopal, I'll tell you. Give him one chance. After all, he's one of our own,' G.S. Rao said. Venugopal sat back, looking from G.S. Rao to Mohan Babu who had shifted to the edge of his seat.

'I will clear out all these wrong-doers saar. I'll reduce ten per cent of the workforce, bring defects down to one per cent. Give me six months.'

G.S. Rao nodded and Venugopal shook his head. 'Don't fail me this time, because if you do, it'll be your end,' he said with a menacing look in his eyes.

'Forgive me, saar,' Mohan Babu said, bowing his head in shame and prostrating before G.S. Rao and Venugopal Reddy.

■

'What do you think?' a beaming Hitesh asked as he leaned against a blue Alto.

'Not too impressed,' Sushma said, sounding indifferent. 'I think you can do a lot better.'

'This is the best car in its class, sir. It has the highest fuel economy at 25 kmpl,' the eager salesman blurted out.

'Yes, I'm sure it is but we aren't interested,' Sushma said in a tone of finality, while Hitesh looked confused. He quietly followed her out of the showroom when she stopped before an SX4, admiringly.

'This looks like the car I'd be proud of,' she said, eyes shining.

'It costs three times as much,' Hitesh said with a frown.

'I've said what I had to say. It's your decision to make.'

They walked over to a café and ordered coffee and snacks.

'I've got a surprise for you,' Hitesh grinned.

'What is that?' she asked, still annoyed.

'I have tickets on Easyfly to Goa for this weekend. I have also got Hotel Vasco booked. It's a package deal. I got the whole thing at a discount of Rs 10,000. Isn't it great?'

Sushma frowned. 'You can go alone on your discount packages. I'm not interested.'

'Why are you upset? I thought you would be happy. I saved money, and I'm taking you on a holiday!'

'Very thoughtful of you,' Sushma said sarcastically. 'But I don't want your discount package trips.'

'But…'

'I can't live like this, Hitesh. I want to be pampered and feel good. I want the good things in life. Here you are, a CPA with five years of experience, who lives and thinks like a clerk. A cup of coffee in a five-star hotel is a big deal for you. Get a life! Please drop me back after this. I'm not in a mood for a film today.'

'Alright,' he said, looking confused.

Sushma was someone who constantly challenged his values and beliefs. He had been brought up on the principle of thrift, something that failed to cut ice with her. Hitesh noticed that her muffin was untouched and the samosa had been ignored, after she nibbled on it for a few seconds. He wondered about Venu Reddy's offer to start the new venture. The point she made about him having years of experience but living like a clerk had hit a raw nerve. He wanted the good things in life too. As they left the café, he turned to have a better look at the SX4 on display in the showroom. Sushma hailed an auto and left in a huff.

CHAPTER 8

Hitesh walked in to see G.S. Rao and Venugopal Reddy engaged in an animated conversation on Venugopal's plush sofa.

'Come, come, Hitesh,' Venugopal said jovially.

'Namaste, Minister Sir. Hello, sir.'

'So what are the plans, young man? What have you decided?' Venugopal jumped straight to the topic, while lighting a cigar. G.S. Rao stared at him from the corner of his eye.

'Sir, I'm ready to join this venture. I will help you build it, and take it forward, sir.'

'Very good,' G.S. Rao wheezed. 'The youth are the future of the country, Venu,' he added and stopped, as if he remembered that he was not standing before his audience, giving a speech.

'Very well then, how do you plan to go about this?' Venugopal asked.

'I will resign from my current job, once I go back to office. We can meet next week; I'll have the business plan ready. We can start putting the plans in action while I serve my notice period.'

'Very good! Didn't I tell you, Rao Saar?' Venugopal exclaimed with childlike glee.

'Yes, yes, very smart,' Rao added for effect.

Hitesh stood up to leave when Venugopal gestured to him. 'Why don't you make a trip to Pondicherry this weekend? I have a nice beach house there. I will get the arrangement done. Take a break; you work too hard.'

'Thank you, sir.'

'Remember to take the details from Payal on your way out,' Venugopal said, before turning his attention to the minister, who was also puffing on a cigar.

■

Hitesh knocked before he entered Sahil's little cabin. 'Haan yaar, come in. These days you've been leaving around seven. What happened? Not well or what?'

'Office hours are till six,' Hitesh said, keeping a straight face.

'Hmm... There are a couple of new projects that I want you to take up. You'll have to manage and execute it all by yourself; there is no staff available. And you'll have to go back to your favourite Vizag.'

'Sahil, I'm leaving the firm. Here's my resignation letter.'

'What?' Sahil almost screamed, utterly shocked. 'Don't mess with me; there is a lot of work. I told you the promotion will take six months, didn't I?

'I'm not interested. According to the number of leaves I have left, I need to serve twenty days before I quit, beginning from today. Please accept this...'

'Where are you going? RSG? KPRL? Or joining that BPO, First Wing? Even I got an offer from there. Why do you want to leave, yaar? Relax, have a little patience! Chill maar, thand rak.'

'No Sahil, I'm not moving to any of those,' Hitesh answered calmly.

'Then? US? Canada? Singapore? Dubai, I guess?'

'Sahil, I'm joining a new company. It's a foreign investment. I can't discuss anymore at this stage.'

'Hmm... Think about it, yaar. Why leave? When I get kicked upstairs, you'll have my job,' Sahil said. He paused a moment and offered, 'What if I get your promotion done now with twenty per cent increment?'

'Sahil, the offer I have is one you can't match.'

'Oh, really? And how much is that? They are giving you a horse, is it?' he snickered.

'They're giving me more than what you make; much more, in fact,' Hitesh replied coolly, at which Sahil recoiled and went red in the face.

'Can you finish these two assignments before you go?'

'I can finish one, the one in Hyderabad. I won't be working double shifts; I don't need to.'

'What about the other one?'

'You do that. I'm sure you'll manage.'

'Don't you owe me that much?' Sahil asked angrily.

'No, I don't!'

Hitesh left the cabin and reached his desk, and spent the next few hours absorbed in work. Soon his colleagues began coming up to him. They had heard of his brief altercation with Sahil. His back was patted, and he was given the respect accorded to a hero.

■

At half-past seven, he strode into the hotel, and walked up to Sushma's desk. She greeted him icily and turned to look at the computer screen.

'What are your plans for the evening?' Hitesh asked slowly.

'I have no plans. I'll go home and cook, eat and sleep. Why, do you have discount coupons for Pizza Hut?'

He handed her an envelope. 'What is this?' she asked, sounding uninterested.

'Kingfisher first-class tickets to Pondicherry for this weekend. I have a bungalow by the beach arranged for us,' he said with a smile.

'Oh! If I could hug you here, I would. Hitesh, you're so sweet,' she said, ecstatic, glimmer in the eyes and pearly whites on full display.

'Thank you. Now let's leave, we have reservations at the Shahi Darbar in thirty minutes.'

'Wow, and what are we celebrating?'

'My release from the Smith & Donald prison, and our new SX4,' he said coyly, putting the keys on the table before her.

She covered her mouth with her palms, and tears rolled down her cheeks, as Hitesh's face wore a satisfied smile. He had done it; he had finally managed to make her proud of him.

CHAPTER 9

'So, was it a refreshing break?' Venugopal asked, showing keen interest.

'It was very good. Thank you, sir.'

'Very good. Suresh has left the company, and some of the funds he had misappropriated have been returned. The rest I will discuss later with you, when we're alone.'

'No problem, sir,' Hitesh smiled as Mehta flipped through the pages of the business plan.

'This is splendid! You anticipate profits in the second year itself. This is a very lucrative business indeed,' Venugopal beamed.

'Yes it is, if we manage to get the franchisee network moving soon. Although, in a conservative scenario, it may even take up to four years, to make some profit.'

'Is it?' Venugopal said. 'But we should aim for the aggressive scenario: profit in year one.'

'We can try, but that depends on a lot of factors.'

'You tell me what you need; I'm giving you full control. I've also got Varun Rao to work on this side by side, scouting for potential franchisee partners.'

'The investment, sir; we need at least thirty crores. We need to advertise, invest in systems and processes, contracts in key areas, and a lot of public relations support.'

'Yes, yes. Done! This is a joint investment by the Minsterji and me. We'll route the funds through Channel Islands, for you know...' he said, clearing his throat while Hitesh nodded along. He felt a bit uncomfortable, aware that the investment in the company would come from slush funds brought in by the minister.

'When do you think we can go operational?' Mehta asked.

'I would say six months, minimum.'

'No. This has to move faster, much faster,' Mehta said in a raised voice.

'But we need to get the franchisee network in place, win contracts, put systems and processes...'

'The company is in a precarious position, Hitesh. We are running out of cash, and no one is buying cars. We are paying salaries through the rent we are earning from the housing department,' Mehta said, while Venugopal shifted in his chair.

'Get it up and running within a month from joining. Outsource as much as you can; do what it takes. Work overtime, and get Varun to start signing up franchisees today,' Venugopal said in tone of finality as Hitesh nodded along.

■

Hitesh entered the mall and walked towards the food court, where Rajesh and Sachin were waiting for him.

'Here comes the hero! Where have you been, saala?' Rajesh spoke as soon as he saw Hitesh. Rajesh and Sachin were Hitesh's close friends since school, the only friends he had ever had in fact. Rajesh was the most flamboyant of them; the only heir to his family's flourishing saree business, he had not continued his education after school. Hitesh secretly admired him for having dated a number of pretty girls.

'I had just been a little too tied up with work. How have you guys been?' Hitesh asked smilingly.

'Life is as messy as ever. I'm being sent to the US again. I am just tired of this fucking programming job; having to stay three months away from home, every time I go on such trips, which makes Sudha unhappy. She finds it difficult to stay with my parents all by herself,' said Sachin. He had been the most studious amongst the three in school; Hitesh and he used to spend hours solving mathematics problems together. After school got over, he went on to study at IIT, and began a flourishing career with an American software major that had set up a huge campus in Hyderabad.

'Yaar, stop cribbing. You're living a very relaxed life unlike me, who is forced to run a saree shop, or Hitesh who works double shift on audit assignments. But do look at your waist size; start jogging, dude!'

'I quit, a few days back,' Hitesh broke in, looking around the food court and wondering what to order.

'What? Congrats, yaar!' Rajesh said, looking jubilant.

'That's a surprise! Where are you going?' Sachin asked, before biting into his burger.

'There is this new venture, backed by foreign investors. It's a car rental service. They want me to run the thing. It's the job of a CEO!'

'Wow! Fantastic! This is the new economy for you, the new India! Yaar, find me an investor too. I'll leave my father's old saree shop and start a new business; maybe a designer lingerie store,' Rajesh said, looking excited and chomping on his sandwich.

'You won't ever change! But you have no experience in this business, babu,' the risk-averse Sachin added.

'It's a great business idea. Let's see,' a confident Hitesh said.

'By the way, you are looking different today. Nice shirt. Bought it in a sale or what? Looks expensive,' asked Rajesh, sizing Hitesh up with newfound admiration.

'No, not in a sale; picked it up from the Zodiac store. Anyway, let's get out of here and go to Taj Banjara for coffee. I'll take you for a spin in my new set of wheels,' he smiled, as Rajesh and Sachin looked surprised. They had always associated their good friend with overtimes at work; weird, old-fashioned shirts; and his trademark Hero Honda 125-cc motorcycle.

Hitesh's phone rang; it was Sushma at the other end. 'Yes, the guys will be joining me. We are reaching the café in twenty minutes,' Hitesh said smilingly, before hanging up. 'It's Sushma. Remember the girl in junior college? We are sort of going out.' Rajesh and Sachin gaped at him with a mix of shock and disbelief.

'Good going, dude!' Rajesh exclaimed.

'What are you up to these days?' a baffled Sachin asked, before he removed his pair of glasses and cleaned them with a tissue.

CHAPTER 10

Hitesh moved around with a sense of purpose on his second day in the new job. Super Cabs had leased a swanky new office in the recently completed Zenith Towers on Raj Bhavan Road, a short distance from the Supreme Motors headquarters. Mehta was closely involved with the progress, and handled issues related to the company set up and registration. He had moved a dozen of his more capable staff in Finance, Accounts, Legal and Administration to the new company. Varun had begun efforts in signing up franchisees, and eight of the twenty franchisees were already on board.

Hitesh turned on his laptop that was connected to the projector. He was joined by Mehta, Varun Rao and three other executives, who had come on board as subordinates to him, to lead efforts in Marketing, Public Relations and Customer Services.

'So gentlemen, we're all set to roll out in twenty days. Before we begin, Varun, can you update us on where the franchisees stand in fleet procurement?' Hitesh asked, standing at the head of the table.

'They're progressing well. They've already paid up to procure twenty-five vehicles each, as per the agreed plan. I've instructed the plant on the CNG kit-fitting and the painting of the cars. We have placed orders for the meters and the GPS as well. So things are on track,' Varun said. He seemed more focused and cooperative than Hitesh had imagined.

'This is good, Varun. Mr Mehta, could you please follow up with the production unit regularly, to ensure that things are on track and the orders met?' Hitesh said, turning to Mehta.

'I am following up. The vehicles are ready, only CNG fitting and a paint job remains. I will be going down to the plant next week to supervise the delivery of the first fifty cars. Mohan Babu has assured me that things are on track,' Mehta said. The new company had become his highest priority, and he seemed energized to deliver.

'This is fantastic, gentlemen. Many thanks for your efforts. Now here's the plan: we launch services in Hyderabad, Vizag and Chandigarh on the same day,' Hitesh said, flashing a map of the three cities on the screen. 'Vijay has prepared a press release, and once the fleet is here, we'll have pictures as well. Popular actors Vijay Kumar and Ramya Shekar will be present at the launch in Hyderabad and Vizag. In Chandigarh, we've managed to get Chetan Singh, the test cricketer.'

'I have also got support in place from Talktel, to send out bulk SMSs through our customer service number in these cities. We will be making radio announcements too,' Mahinder, the marketing executive said.

'We will be getting full page spreads in all the leading English and regional dailies. A couple of news channels have confirmed the slots for an interview with Hitesh,' said Sohail, the PR executive.

'We also have hoardings and billboards across these cities, at the airports, with the image of the cab, our customer care number and a catchy jingle,' said Sukanya, the customer service head.

'Yes, we have a bunch of advertisements such as "Flight at 4 a.m.? No problem, call Super Cabs at 800xxxx". Here is another one: "Heavy rain and no autorickshaw? Call Super Cabs at 800xxxx. We'll reach you in thirty minutes. Fast and Friendly."' Hitesh scrolled from one storyboard to another.

'This is very good, Hitesh. Your team has done very well,' Mehta said. Hitesh looked relieved. He had worked like a beaver on weekends with the new team and the ad agency to get things moving.

'Thanks, Mr Mehta. Ten days after this launch we move to Coimbatore, Vijaywada and Madurai. A week after this, Mysore, Mangalore and Ludhiana will follow,' Hitesh said, continuing with a slide on each city that mentioned the population, income statistics and details of flights per day, number of vehicles and other details.

'We will also have our airport counter operational in Mangalore, Vizag, Hyderabad, Coimbatore and Chandigarh in two-three weeks' time from the launch,' Varun Rao added. He had received tacit instructions to get this done at any cost. Venugopal knew that he was the right man to work the red tape, and move things in the direction they desired.

'I have another suggestion,' Hitesh added. 'I would like the franchisees to drive their entire fleet like a procession through key localities in each of these cities. It will definitely create a buzz.'

'Good idea,' Varun Rao smiled.

'Thanks. This has been a very successful meeting. We will meet again next week. Keep up the good work,' Mehta said, before he requested Hitesh to join him separately, for a one on one meeting.

'Let's hope all these ideas work,' Varun Rao said, while walking out with Hitesh. 'The franchisees are an impatient lot. They would want to see quick returns,' he concluded with a wry smile, Hitesh looking a tad exhausted as he walked out behind him.

■

'Your CEO son is finally home,' Hitesh's father said, as he switched channels from one political debate to another.

Hitesh sat down, loosened the collar button and removed the tie. He looked up at the ceiling fan that whirred, moving at a slow speed.

'It's time we have an air conditioner at home,' Hitesh muttered.

'Yes. Please go and buy one and fix it. Just like you went and bought a new car without asking me. You're a big man now. What can I say?'

'You stop troubling my son, Ji,' his mother protested. 'He is working very hard these days. Come beta, your dinner is ready.'

'Working hard or roaming around with some loose woman? Desai saw him walk into some jeweller's store in Banjara Hills with some girl,' his father said, staring at him angrily.

'I'm old enough to go out with whoever I choose to. I'm not spending your money, am I?' Hitesh asked defiantly.

'Okay enough. Stop this argument now. Hitesh beta, your uncle called up today. We can still talk to Dimple's father, and fix a wedding date. She is very good—traditional and homely. What do you say, beta?'

'Ma, I'm tired after a hectic day at work. And I am more tired of you people's sarcasm and pestering. I don't want to marry that dumb Dimple. Not in this lifetime or the next!'

'Happy?' his father asked the mother angrily, before he switched off the television.

'Okay, no problem. There is also that girl Priya. She is very beautiful, and is from a good family. She broke her engagement with this boy from Mumbai when they came to know of his philandering ways. He is a banker. Tell me, should I talk? You're a big executive now. You drive such a nice car too...'

'Ma, I told you I'm tired of this! Whenever I wish to get married, I'll let you know. I'll also introduce you to the girl. Till then, you relax and look after your health. Don't worry about my marriage, for God's sake!'

Tears rolled down his mother's cheeks, and an irritated Hitesh stopped eating and stood up.

'Here, look at me, Hitesh. Don't forget that you're still a child and this is our house. Now apologize to your mother and go meet this Priya on the weekend. We will forgive you for all that you've been up to recently,' his father said firmly.

'If this is your house, I'm leaving right now. I can't take this anymore. I'm just tired of being ordered around all my life!' He barged into his room, and began packing a rucksack.

'Yes, go from here. You think you're a big man because you work for that playboy, Venugopal Reddy? We live in a respectable society; we don't want a loafer of a son. We'll manage,' his father hollered, while his mother looked deeply worried.

'It's okay, beta. Don't marry now. Where are you going?' his mother pleaded.

'Don't stop me, Ma. I'm suffocated in this house. I'll come and take my remaining things on the weekend. You look after yourself,' he said, touching her feet and heading towards the front door. He refused to meet the angry gaze of his father who stood there with a deep frown.

Fifteen minutes later, Hitesh rang the bell outside Rajesh's apartment. He had sent him a text message before getting into his car.

'Come in, dost. Sorry, but my father wants you to leave in two days. I have unmarried sisters at home, and a building full of pesky neighbours,' Rajesh said hesitantly on opening the door.

'That's okay. I'll find something by tomorrow evening. Sushma is taking a day off to look for an apartment for me,' he said, walking towards Rajesh's room with a rucksack on his shoulder.

CHAPTER 11

Hitesh stood nervously before the camera as the microphone was thrust before him. He cleared his throat and began. 'We have just launched a service which is built on the model of cooperative dairy farming in the country. We have one service that will be operated in twenty cities, but that will be owned by franchisees. We are giving the power to the common man, and this is a big step in encouraging empowerment and entrepreneurship,' Hitesh said with increasing confidence.

The camera moved over to the celebrities who smiled for the shutterbugs and posed next to the fleet that had been lined up. The media had covered the celebrities driving up from their houses in Jubilee Hills to the Super Cabs office on Raj Bhavan Road.

'Cab service now powered by the youth'—read the ticker on the regional news channels. The print journalists gushed over Hitesh: a young accountant, who came from a middle-class background, now spearheaded the new company that aimed to revolutionize taxi services in India.

Venugopal stood in the background and kept a low profile. He was asked to give sound bites for a couple of news channels. 'We encourage and support entrepreneurship. Super Cabs is a combination of youthful energy and heritage. Supreme Motors has been in this country for generations, and we will supply the fleet for this new company all over the country, to every franchisee. We will also support the repairs, servicing and maintenance from the centres we've set up nationwide,' he said proudly.

'This is a big day for the youth of our state. We have created a model that will create thousands of jobs nationwide,' Minister

G.S. Rao said as he joined the celebrities on their inaugural run in the city.

'We don't know how they'd make money at the fares they are reported to charge,' a representative from Heinz Cabs said with some scepticism.

'It's a good idea, but we wonder how profitable it would be, given that the fleet is entirely composed of the gas-guzzling heritage models from Supreme Motors. The cars will spend more time at the service station than on the road,' another from Axis Car Rental chuckled.

Hitesh refuted these charges in the media the next day. 'We aim to end the era of overpriced car rental services. We are taking cab services to ordinary people in cities where public transportation is weak and unreliable. We are surprised to see some who are grudging and dismissing our heritage and culture. We'll prove them wrong.'

Long reports were written about the new company's commitment to support the local industries, and to create jobs for those who are unemployed. Some newspapers even had editorials praising Hitesh's patriotic values, castigating executives of MNC rental agencies, as foreign agents making money for Americans. Hitesh's PR campaign had a successful start, which hit a high note on the company's arrival in Mysore and Ludhiana. State chief ministers showed up to inaugurate the service, some calling it the 'people's car service'.

Hitesh hit another masterstroke by getting the franchisees to recruit former auto drivers for Super Cabs, after proper training. Their stories were published in local newspapers and magazines, on how this was a positive change in their lives. He received calls and requests for meetings from ministers in Karnataka, Jharkhand, Gujarat, Maharashtra and Chattisgarh, to roll out franchisees in their cities.

Hitesh travelled every single day; he would be present at every launch, at times with Varun Rao and Mahinder, the marketing executive, in tow. He met franchisees, local politicians and businessmen; he spoke tirelessly to the media who lapped him up as a youth icon for the middle class, and oversaw the roll-out of the services from close quarters.

'What's the response you're getting from the franchisees?' Hitesh asked Varun Rao, as they waited for their luggage to arrive at the airport.

'Very good; they are getting good business, boss. The billing system shows eighty per cent utilization, on an average. There are some problems though; some vehicles required servicing early on; a couple had to be sent back. We'll have to manage production closely, as we need to supply the second run of the fleet and minimize production defects.'

'I agree,' a contemplative Hitesh said. The only weak link here were the jaded models of Supreme Motors, but he had tried to combat that by harping on their culture, heritage and the support of local enterprise. 'We've also got some customer complaints on the attitude of some drivers. You'll need to get behind franchisees on that one. Customer care is the key,' he emphasized as Varun Rao nodded along, keeping his eyes on the conveyor belt.

Hitesh's attention turned to the television screen. A business news channel was showing a graph, highlighting the share price of Supreme Motors. The price had shot up by 1,000 per cent over the last two months, and was trading at Rs 50 per share, as opposed to the previous Rs 5. Mehta appeared briefly on the screen and spoke about how the company had reinvented itself as the supplier to car rental agencies. He claimed that the company had sales orders from a dozen other car rental agencies similar to Super Cabs, but was focusing mostly on their key customers. Exports to car rental agencies in Nepal and Bangladesh were in the pipeline.

A nervous Mohan Babu appeared on the screen as well, with a picture of the company's assembling unit in the background. 'We are implementing the best practices in our units with the hope to cut out defects significantly. We have increased production by thirty per cent using the same resources,' he pointed out.

Varun Rao smiled to himself as Hitesh dragged his trolley bag, seemingly in an upbeat mood. They both walked up to the Super Cabs counter and stood in the line for their turn, wanting to assess the service themselves.

'We have twelve franchisees now,' Varun Rao said. 'We need to sign a few more by next month. There is a lot of interest; I'm meeting a few people in Bangalore and Chennai this week, and am off to Delhi next week.'

'That's good; keep things moving along fast. Venugopal wants the rest signed by the end of next month,' Hitesh added as he browsed through the emails on his new smartphone.

'Hmm… Let's aim to do that. I'll get the bid evaluation process into fast track.'

■

Hitesh kept his gaze fixed on Sushma as she sipped from the glass of wine. She looked stunning, wearing the diamond earrings he had gifted her. Her gaze met his, and she smiled at him dreamily.

'When do you get back?' she asked. Hitesh was about to leave the city for a few days, to attend a strategy workshop at Stanford. Sushma was now pretty much living in with him; she visited her own apartment only a couple of times in a week. She had decorated his apartment tastefully, something Hitesh had appreciated and was proud of. She had even coaxed Hitesh to invite his parents for dinner. They came. Though they winced at the subtle signs in the house suggesting the presence of a woman, they could not hide their awe and pride for their son who had reached further ahead than they had ever imagined, rather quickly.

'In a week; it's just a three-day workshop. But I plan to stay on for a couple of days, and do some shopping for you.' She smiled coyly. Hitesh felt satisfied that he had been able to live up to Sushma's desires and expectations. After things had warmed between him and his parents after their visit to his apartment, he had introduced them to Sushma. They all met at a restaurant. To Hitesh's great relief, his parents had rather liked her, and Sushma too met them cordially.

'I'll probably take your mum shopping in the meanwhile,' she said. She now drove his SX4, as he had been given a company-owned Supreme Passion, a revved-up sports version of the vintage model.

'Sushma, I was thinking…' Hitesh leaned forward, cleared his throat and continued, 'Let's get married.' He spoke softly, aware of the people around who were engaged in animated conversations. Old Hindi melodies played in the background, setting the relaxed ambience at the dimly lit Golden Chimney restaurant at the Sheraton.

'Hitesh! Stop it!' she said, looking embarrassed. 'Don't spoil the mood. Just enjoy.'

'But what is wrong? We are practically living together. I'm a simple guy, Sushma. I want marriage…'

'I want it too, Hitesh. But I need time to think. I want to be sure, to be ready for it. Right now, you're settled and I'm happy about it. But I'm not happy and settled in my own line of work; I work at the reception in a hotel, while I really want to act. I don't want to give up my dreams, Hitesh. I hope you understand…'

'So you won't marry me…' Hitesh said, looking dejected.

'Not now! Let's not talk about it,' she said. They continued to eat in silence and left the restaurant after a few minutes.

She got into the car next to him. They sat silently for a while after which Hitesh removed a small gift-wrapped box from the dashboard. 'This is for you,' he said, in a pensive mood, before handing it to her.

She quietly took the box and opened it. Inside was a diamond-studded Omega watch. She removed it and put it on her wrist, while tears rolled down her cheeks.

'Oh Hitesh...' she said, and leaned in and began kissing him passionately on his lips. They continued to kiss in the parking lot, but stopped abruptly when they saw the headlights of a car flash as it drove into the basement of the hotel.

'Are you coming home?' he asked, as she adjusted her hair and wiped her lips.

'Of course,' she said with a mischievous smile.

'I love you, Sushma.'

'You're a sweetheart. It's beautiful!' she said.

CHAPTER 12

Hitesh flipped through the customer satisfaction report with rapt attention. His phone rang again; this time it was a professor from his college. His phone had been ringing non-stop since morning, after he returned from the workshop at Stanford. He had been accorded the Young Entrepreneur of the Year award by *Business Planet* magazine, and congratulatory calls and messages had flooded his phone since the news broke out. He was to go and collect the award in a week's time, at a high-end, star-studded ceremony. He planned to take Sushma along. He wanted to pack in as much work as possible before lunch. In the afternoon, he had to give a talk at the Hyderabad School of Business that was developing a case study that featured Super Cabs' business model. In the evening, he had to shoot for the cover of *Yuva* magazine that featured him along with a tennis prodigy and a young film actor.

Hitesh heard a knock on the door and saw Payal peeping in. 'Come in,' he said, eyes fixed back to the laptop screen and continuing to work, 'Mr Mehta asked me to see you. What's happening in Supreme Motors? Why had he requested me to consider a position for you here?'

'Well, you know, thanks to all your good work, Venu is in an upbeat mood. The office now resembles a film set. He's hired a couple of young starlets for office work; one as his personal assistant and another as his receptionist. Even the old office receptionist has been replaced by a younger woman...'

'Is it?' Hitesh interrupted her, surprised, even though he knew of Venugopal's roving eye, and his libido that he found hard to control.

'I never really liked the office atmosphere. I've been spurning his advances for months now. So it's no surprise that he fired me,' she smiled sadly.

'I'm sorry to hear that. How can I help?' Hitesh said, looking at her troubled face. She removed her glasses. Hitesh noticed that behind those thick glasses was a pair of beautiful, dreamy eyes. Payal was very attractive, he thought. He had always appreciated the dignity with which she carried herself, despite working for a man like Venu.

'Honestly, I need the job. I have a family to support. Mr Mehta mentioned that you might need a bit of help; you apparently are stressed and overworked.'

'Sure, Payal. I'm sure you can join us as my assistant. You can manage my mailbox, manage media relations, press releases, my appointments...There's a lot you can help with. Why don't you start tomorrow?'

'Thank you,' she said, relieved, smiling at him and then to herself.

'Welcome aboard,' he said, returning the smile.

■

Sahil walked into the cabin with a nameplate carved on the door 'CEO Hitesh Patel'. He admired the art on the walls and the various photographs hanging on them, framed in glass. Most had Hitesh in the forefront at the launch of Super Cabs. One had him accepting an award, with the employees behind him.

'You've made a lot of progress in a short time, yaar! Who would have thought, huh? Tu toh baap nikla,' he said, managing a friendly smile. Gone was the cocky arrogance of a senior, Hitesh thought.

'How are things at the firm?' Hitesh asked, changing the topic.

'All fine, yaar. Now I'm counting on you for support. Of course you'll be needing support in terms of tax filing, audit, accounting services, etc. Considering that we have worked together before, we were hoping for your business.'

Sahil was not the sort who would beat around the bush. Hitesh smiled at him. 'Yes we do need these services, but we believe in working with local enterprises. So we have signed up Ramesh Babu & Co. and Chaturvedi partners for the purpose,' Hitesh answered calmly.

Sahil felt flushed for a moment, but regained his composure soon. 'Arey yaar, do something, na! There should be some loyalty, no? After all you have spent so many years at the firm!'

'I understand, Sahil, but sorry.'

Sahil nodded and leaned back in the chair. Then, looking at the walls, he said, 'Okay, that girlfriend of yours, Sandra...' Sahil looked at Hitesh now. 'We fired her.' Hitesh was startled, stung by the mere mention of her name. Sahil looked triumphant.

'What happened?'

'Lots of client complaints. She would disappear from the client location for long hours at a stretch. One CFO once called up complaining that her breath reeked of alcohol. She was fired on disciplinary grounds.'

'Yes, she was a difficult girl.'

Then a wicked smile appeared on Sahil's face. 'You know, in her exit interview, she rattled on about how you pursued her, kissed her and called her at odd hours. She tried to insinuate charges of sexual exploitation against you. I asked her to shut up and take a recommendation later and go. I shredded the transcript from that conversation. It's not good, you know, all that stuff going in a file.' Sahil shrugged his shoulders, and stared at Hitesh.

Hitesh, who had kept his cool until now, looked visibly disturbed. 'Well, there's little truth in such allegations...' he said, sounding worried.

'Yes, yes, she kept mentioning some pictures of her you had that you had used to blackmail her. But don't get agitated; I've taken care of it. I even gave her a recommendation for a job in a BPO. I'm not judging you; shit happens. I understand you; we are friends.'

'Thanks. I have to leave for a meeting now,' Hitesh said, uneasily shifting in his chair.

'Sure yaar. Busy man you are! Anyway, tell me, is there an opening for a CFO in Super Cabs? Maybe I can come in. We are friends; I work for you or you work for me, it is the same thing, no?' Sahil's crooked smile had just become wider. Was it this cunning and shrewdness of Sahil that had earned him promotions every year, and a chance to hobnob with the big bosses in the company? Hitesh cringed and decided that he would never turn to such scheming ways to rise in his career.

'Hmm…There's no such requirement at this point, but I'll keep you in mind if the need arises,' he answered.

'Thanks, yaar. It was good seeing you, and it's nice to see Supreme Motors doing so well in the stock market. I got my father to buy shares too. Tell me, is Venugopal offloading a part of his stake? You're an insider, aren't you? Give me some tip-off yaar,' he said with a wink.

'I have no clue,' Hitesh said hurriedly, standing up and shaking Sahil's hand to indicate that the meeting was over. He needed to be careful of Sahil. The revelations had left him cold.

■

Hitesh entered the conference room where Mahinder was already deep in discussion with Sohail and Sukanya.

'How are things? I've been getting mixed reports from Varun Rao. The numbers are static; we aren't seeing the organic growth we had expected. I'm hoping for your feedback, as you are more in touch with what's going on,' Hitesh said.

'There's a bit of a problem with how different franchisees work. Many of them have drivers without multilingual skills. Some of the drivers, particularly the low-paid, are quite new to the job, and don't know the roads and localities well. This is particularly the case in the South,' Mahinder said.

'We also have a couple of incidents that have generated bad PR: one driver in Chandigarh brawled with a customer who had abused him; in Madurai, there was an instance of eve-teasing by the driver; and an unfortunate accident occurred in Indore, where the driver was speeding,' Sohail said, looking at some clippings before him.

'This is similar to the nature of the feedback we get from the drivers in the call centres. We've been told that our drivers are rude and stubborn; they fail to return change; and sometimes even get into heated arguments,' Sukanya added.

'This is the problem when one grows at the pace we have,' Hitesh said. 'Sukanya, commence an etiquette training course and a manual for all franchisees. This will be implemented over the next two months. We'll get mystery shoppers to pose as customers; each driver will be assessed against set parameters. Those failing will be given a month to improve. After this, you will commission a survey via an SMS sent to each registered customer. In three months, we should aim for standardization and better service.'

'Good idea, Hitesh,' Sukanya said as she took down notes.

'Sohail, send out press releases to the key media people in each city; emphasize on the driver training and orientation programme. Also, begin a policy of twenty-five per cent discount for senior citizens, between 11 a.m. and 4 p.m. We'll communicate this to the franchisees.' He turned to Sukanya. 'We need to focus on safety in the training. It's mandatory that seat belts are used and speed limits are adhered to by the drivers. Maybe we can do free ads on the sides of the cars for a month, supporting safe driving.'

'Yes. The police departments in all the cities will be happy with this,' Sohail said.

'I think we need a bit of advertising, Hitesh. I'm not sure we have the budget, but reaching out to a wider audience through advertisements on TV is the key,' Mahinder said.

'You're right. Heinz Cabs has begun advertising in Hyderabad and Chennai. There's also a recent upstart called Fast Cabs, who've imitated our business model. They are operational in three of the cities we are in, and they use a better fleet—Ford Ikons,' Sukanya said.

'Let's arrange the cost for advertisements from within our budget; let's aim for print ads, TVCs, a new radio jingle and some online banners.' Hitesh nodded. Then, sipping his coffee, he said, 'Maybe getting a young woman as a brand ambassador would help.'

'That might work! Let me talk to the agency,' Mahinder beamed.

'Good. Let's meet after a week and see the progress in these initiatives.' Hitesh concluded the meeting before he checked his phone and got busy with it. Sushma had sent him a text message asking if they were going out for dinner.

CHAPTER 13

Hitesh and Varun Rao entered Venugopal's cabin after being greeted by his temptress of a secretary. Varun had felt awkward as they waited at the reception while the girl, wearing a dress too small for an office, that clearly showed her ample cleavage, confirmed the meeting with her boss. Varun had given her more than a passing glance and whispered in Hitesh's ear, 'Venu seems to be reliving his youth these days, huh? I hear he's passed on his old secretary to you. How is she?' Hitesh hadn't liked the question. 'She's a good girl. Very efficient at her work,' he had replied in a business-like manner.

'I like efficient women,' Varun Rao had said with his wolfish grin, and fixed his gaze on Venu's secretary. They were asked to go in and wait for Venu. Now they sat waiting inside while Hitesh still looked uncomfortable.

Venugopal joined them a few minutes later, followed by Mehta, who appeared out of breath.

'Sorry, gentlemen; I had gone out to meet the CII president for breakfast; they are very impressed with our efforts. Did you see the news in the morning? Our share price is hovering at Rs 95. I'm putting up eighty per cent of my stake, which adds up to thirty-five per cent of the equity, up for a public offering. I expect that it would be oversubscribed. The tailwind is with us. Now tell me, where have we reached with the franchisees?'

'Sixteen done, four more to go,' Varun Rao said, before Hitesh interrupted him.

'Fourteen actually, I'm yet to approve two,' Hitesh said.

'Hmm…Hitesh, let me be candid with you. I need you people to move quickly. I want twenty-five franchisees instead of twenty. I believe we have the infrastructure in place for it,' Venugopal said as he swung his arms.

'I think we need to slow things down a bit, Venu,' Hitesh said.

'Why? What for?' Venugopal was in a combative mood. Mr Mehta sat back, looking morose.

'We are trying to fix issues in services, Venu. There are issues like cars' breakdown; customer complaints; service standards are not clear and, in some cases, aren't even being implemented; a driver-mentoring programme is underway. All of this will take six months to settle.'

'But this is with the existing franchisees, Hitesh. We can keep running these improvement programmes, and sign new franchisees on the side,' Varun chimed in.

'We don't have clear standards for them to follow; there are customer service issues and policy gaps. We are currently busy trying to solve this. It's a distraction…'

'If you are busy, I can go ahead and sign franchisees if I have the authority. I have a party who is willing to take five franchisees in the Northeast and Eastern region today, if we agree to drop our share to twenty per cent of the takings. They feel there are higher operating costs in these parts,' Varun Rao explained, keeping his gaze on Venugopal, who seemed ecstatic.

'Go ahead, Varun Garu. I'm giving you the authority. Sign this party on. It's important to see a spike in sales at Supreme Motors. I'll have the plant working over time. I want the price at Rs 125 per share when I sell. The market is hot,' Venugopal hollered. 'Hitesh, you don't worry. Work on service improvement. Varun will bring in the franchisees.'

'But Venu, the risk of giving all this to one party, and that too on terms different than what the rest have agreed to, is a huge risk! I will have to think about it. On one side there's Supreme Motors, and on the other we need to support the fledgling Super Cabs, and focus on its long-term reputation.'

Mehta smiled wryly, first at Varun Rao then at Venugopal Reddy. 'You send me your recommendations, Hitesh. I will think and decide upon a course of action. I hear you're planning to advertise in a big way? Very good,' Venugopal beamed.

'He is a very effective leader,' Mehta added weakly, as Varun Rao nodded reluctantly.

'Alright, gentlemen, I will convene a meeting soon. Varun, leave the proposed agreements with Hazel, my secretary.' He turned to Hitesh. 'There's another personal matter that I need your advice on. Maybe you can stay on and we can talk.'

'Of course, Venu.' Varun Rao smiled at him cautiously before he left the room. He knew that Hitesh was sharp, and, thanks to him, even the likes of Vinod and Suresh had got into a spot of bother. He contemplated a meeting to discuss the Northeast proposal with Hitesh once again before he sent it to Venu.

CHAPTER 14

Hitesh woke up with a start and checked his Blackberry. It was half past seven. He turned to look at Sushma, who was sleeping next to him. Her long, soft tresses covered her face. She was wearing nothing but a pair of hot pants. They had had a late night; a birthday party hosted by the head of Hyderabad Bank for his wife. Hitesh was often invited to such parties these days, and he attended whichever ones he considered important enough.

He leaned back in the bed and, removing strands of her hair, kissed her on her lips.

'What time is it?' she asked, sounding sleepy, with her eyes shut.

'An hour before you go to work.' He ran his fingers down her neck and fondled her supple breasts.

'Hm…Don't trouble me. I have to get up in five minutes.'

'Yes you have to, love. It's probably your last day at work,' he said softly.

She sat up and covered her ample bosom with the sheet. He was smiling. 'Why do you have to start this again?' she asked, annoyed. They had been bickering lately about her job. He wanted her to quit her job, which he found demeaning, given his position, while she wanted to remain independent.

He moved behind her and kissed softly on her shoulder and bare back. He played with her hair and ran his lips down to the small of her back, kissing her barbed wire tattoo.

'Okay, time to get ready for work,' she said, pushing his hand away to look for her T-shirt.

'Wait,' he said, putting his arms around her and drawing her close with a little force. He kissed her on the neck. 'I have some good news for you,' he grinned.

'And what's that?'

'We are shooting for an ad in Mumbai for the next couple of days. I'm leaving tonight.'

'What's so good about it? I should get ready,' she said, again looking for her clothes between the sheets, as he moved his fingers down to her navel.

'The good thing is that you're featuring in it. You'll be on TV, in the papers and on billboards across the country. So go quit that job and come home soon.'

'What? I can't believe this!' she shrieked, and turned around, one hand covering her mouth. 'You're not joking, right? But how? How could this be? No audition?'

'Don't worry; I had it all arranged. I gave the ad agency the portfolio we shot for you, and they said, quite clearly, you are the one they want for their campaign!'

'Oh, Hitesh! You're such a darling! I'm so happy!' She looked like an overjoyed schoolgirl at that moment, having let down her guard, standing naked in all her vulnerability. She put her arms around him, and kissed his lips.

'I'm going to make sure this takes you places,' he said, caressing her back as she hugged him tightly, eyes far away. Hitesh remembered how he had cut a deal with the ad agency to allow her to model. He was glad that his little lie had made her feel so happy about herself. Maybe this breakthrough would fulfil her dreams, and make her ready for marriage, he thought. They lay back in bed as he thrust himself inside her and moaned with anticipation. He wrapped his arms around her and she dug her nails into his back, heaving and groaning in pleasure.

'It's everything I've waited for, Hitesh. Thank you,' she said.

■

'So you're out to shoot the ad, huh?' Varun Rao asked.

'I should be gone for a couple of days.'

'I wanted you to finalize these contracts for Delhi and the Northeast before you go. They're fine; please sign them,' he said, thrusting the bunch of papers before him. 'Standard terms, except the sharing of revenues with our friends in the Northeast.'

'That's what I'm wary about. What if the others learn of it? It could be a disaster for our public relations with other franchisees! We are also trying to support local enterprise. Why offer three franchisees to the Delhi party, and all five in the region to the guys in the East?'

'Well, see Hitesh, it makes a lot of sense. I have to deal with the franchisees; it's a lot less headache dealing with one instead of ten. There will be bigger, well-managed operations.'

'I don't want the business to lose leverage.'

'It won't. You heard the boss's instruction. He wants so many more signed; it's a couple of months before he offloads his stake.'

'Leave the contract papers with me; I'll give these back to you once I return,' Hitesh said. 'It is important to consider all factors before making a decision.'

■

There was a call on Hitesh's intercom; it was Payal. 'Sir, it's Mr Mathur, the franchisee owner from Ludhiana.'

'Put him on,' Hitesh said, sounding busy.

'Haanji, Hitesh Sir. How are you doing?'

'Good. Thanks, Mr Mathur. And you?'

'Sir, I have a problem. This twenty-five per cent remittance to you out of the total billing is too much. The CNG prices have shot up, while the fares are fixed, which makes difficult to get more drivers and, to top that, we invariably have a car or two in the garage for servicing.'

'I'm not sure what can be done. This is a company policy. We could look at reviewing the fares in six months, based on market rates and our position.'

'No, but the current rate of twenty-five per cent is anyway too much. You should bring it down.'

'I'm afraid that this isn't possible, Mr Mathur. Although I have something that might help you: we could do a lot of ads on the sides of the cars in your fleet. We have many such requests.'

'Hmm… Alright. But do consider what I requested. We operate under pressure here, paying ministers, police and, at times, our competitor's employees.'

'I understand, although it's difficult to change company policy.'

Hitesh hung up, and turned on the business news channel and saw that the Supreme Motors stock was rallying at Rs 105/ share.

He sat back and thought about the conversation he had just had and stared long and hard at the monitor, before he hesitated for a moment and dialled a friend's number.

CHAPTER 15

Hitesh stood away from the crowd, with a reporter from the *Himalyan Gazette*. The national cricket star, Rahul Singh, posed for shutterbugs at the launch of Super Cabs' new franchisee in Dehradun. Hitesh had flown into the city soon after the ad shoot in Mumbai, which Sushma had starred in, directed by an upcoming young filmmaker.

'What are your plans for the future? Your company is expanding at a furious pace,' the reporter asked, looking at Hitesh appreciatively as she began to scribble in her notepad.

'We aim to be the biggest cab service in the country in three years, with a fleet of 2,000 vehicles in forty cities. Yes, we are expanding very fast. This brings its own new challenges, but also has its upside.'

'But there have been issues with services as well as complaints from customers in some cities. To add to this, the fleet is entirely composed of an outdated model of Supreme Motors. Is this sustainable? What do you have to say on this?'

'Well, firstly, the Supreme Motors' new model, Passion, is an upgraded vehicle fitted with a CNG kit. We believe it's the right choice. It's helped us keep costs down. In some cities with comparable services, we work at twenty to twenty-five per cent lesser rates than Heinz Car Rental and Axis Cabs. This is *the* game-changer. On service issues, we have a complaint management programme in place. We are running various training and orientation models and we will see considerable service improvement in six months.'

'What about your reliance on franchisees? The business depends on them entirely. On the other hand, you have small-time cab operators setting up shop, and there are some companies banding together to take on you. What do think of the competitive landscape?'

'The franchisee network has helped us build a bigger business than would have been possible otherwise. It's a model that has worked across the globe, to grow and expand business. We are aware of competition and we welcome it; we believe we have the edge.'

'How do you propose to retain the clientele?'

'We are starting a loyalty programme where those who pay Rs 50 for the card will receive a ten per cent discount on the fare across franchisees of Super Cabs. This, we believe, will keep existing customers in the fold.'

'Any comments on the protests by local taxi operators that took place prior to your launch?'

'We are unaware of what motivated it, but we feel that there is enough room for everyone. Our best wishes are with these local people. Thanks.'

'Congratulations on being bestowed the Young Business Leader Award by SNBC Business, sir. Thanks for talking to us.' Hitesh nodded confidently and stepped back towards where the action was.

He returned to the centre-stage where pictures were being taken with Rahul Singh, flanked by the franchise owner. Cricket fans hooted and whistled, waiting in anticipation to speak to the star and, possibly, get clicked with him.

■

As he landed in Mumbai, Hitesh walked out of the airport to see huge hoardings of Super Cabs staring at him. More billboards could be seen every now and then, as the taxi navigated through the peak-hour traffic on the Western Express Highway. Venugopal had got a franchisee to run in Mumbai as well, with the sole aim of gaining visibility with the investors. The franchisee was fronted by a shadow company, managed by one of his handlers.

Hitesh checked his phone to find his inbox filled with messages: congratulations and praises from friends and colleagues. There was one even from Sahil, more a teaser that said, 'Good going! Killing it on all fronts, bandhu. But don't forget your old friends.' Hitesh ignored it and smiled at the success of his advertisement campaign.

He quickly freshened up and changed at a hotel in Juhu, and left for a lounge located in the suburbs, where Sushma had organized a party for her friends from the modelling and film industry—mostly strugglers like her. While Hitesh had been frantically touring cities, Sushma had stayed on in Mumbai to wrap up her print ad assignments and audition for a few modelling opportunities.

Hitesh walked into the lounge and searched for familiar faces. He found none, except, of course, for Sushma who seemed insanely happy, taking one round of tequila shots after the other with her friends, who were merrily drinking away and cheering her on to do the same. He was meeting Sushma after more than a week—the longest they had been away from each other, ever since their surprise meeting at Venu's party six months ago. He sighed in relief and walked towards her. He held her gently from behind and planted a kiss on her cheek. She turned around and smiled, got up from the chair and gave him what Hitesh felt was a businesslike hug and peck on the cheek. He felt a bit disappointed but decided, on looking at her bloodshot eyes, that it must be the drinks. He joined the group for another four rounds and watched Sushma and her friends enjoying themselves till the night of merriment drew to a close. Sushma, who had been putting up at a friend's apartment, left with an inebriated Hitesh for his suite in the five-star hotel in Juhu.

They kissed in the taxi on the way to the hotel, Hitesh hungrily and she a bit reluctantly. In between, he comically kept proposing marriage to her while she whacked his arm away in mock anger.

The next morning, he woke up with a hangover. Sushma was sleeping next to him, looking like an angel. Soon after, sipping his coffee, he skimmed through the business pages in the newspaper when he was shocked out of his wits!

'Super Cabs Signs Six New Franchisees'—read the headline of a small news piece in the lower half of the page. The story had a photograph of Varun Rao and Mehta smiling. 'Varun Rao, the COO of Super Cabs and Mr Mehta, the CFO of Supreme Motors, talk about Super Cabs scaling new heights', read the caption. He noticed the company ad that featured Sushma, which brought only a faint smile to his face.

He dialled Varun Rao's number. Not bothering to greet him, he jumped straight to the question.

'How could you do this? I haven't even signed on these deals! Who gave you the authority to make the announcement?' he screamed.

'Relax, sir,' a calm voice came from the other end. 'I did what Venugopal wanted me to. He did not want to wait. I respect your authority, but his instructions supersede your advice, don't they?' Hitesh smelled a rat. He realized that Varun's intentions weren't good, and that he could sell his soul to whoever called the shots.

He next called Mehta who sounded apologetic. 'Venugopal wanted to move ahead right then. Anyway, you must have seen that our share prices have shot up to Rs 150. Isn't it wonderful? So, how has the advertisement come along? I'm yet to see it.' Hitesh hung up.

Lastly, he diallled Venugopal's number. Venugopal picked up soon and, before Hitesh could say anything, lashed out at him, 'You weren't around to make an important announcement for the company! I had to coach Varun Rao to get it done.'

'I did see the announcement in the paper. But does Supreme Motors have what it takes to meet such an ambitious production schedule?' Hitesh decided not to raise the subject of the new contracts signed in his absence, for he knew Venugopal would be in an inebriated state, given that he always began his day with a few pegs of whisky.

'Don't worry; they'll do as I tell them. I really like the advertisements. Very nice model you've found!' he said before hanging up.

Sushma woke up, groggy and eyes red. He moved closer to her and kissed her, before he ordered a cup of coffee and toast for her. He then showed her the newspaper supplement that featured a full-page advertisement of Super Cabs. Her eyes lit up.

'This is amazing! It's like a bolt from the blue, this whole Super Cabs success. Thanks, Hitesh,' she said, kissing him back.

'Anything for you, love! So how do you want to spend the day? We have a flight at seven, remember?'

'Hmm...Let's go for lunch to Pali Village Café. Actually... Could you extend my stay here by a week? A couple of meetings have come up...possible modelling assignments. You can postpone my ticket till next Friday.'

'Okay. Interesting...I'm happy for you,' he said with some hesitance, as she picked up her phone to receive a call from her newly appointed agent.

CHAPTER 16

G.V. Vinod entered the seedy bar and looked around for a familiar face. A tacky dance number made a jarring sound from the old, worn-out speakers that hung overhead.

He spotted Suresh, dressed in a blue-checked bush-shirt and a pair of black trousers, drinking alone in a dark corner. Vinod went and sat opposite him, giving him a familiar smile. Suresh looked up with his bloodshot eyes and turned his face away.

'Your wife told me that I might find you here,' Vinod said in a friendly voice as Suresh beckoned for two pints of beer. He lit up a Charminar and blew smoke in Vinod's face.

'And what are you doing here in the middle of a working day?' he asked gruffly.

'I…ah, I am being transferred to Hyderabad as the office and administration manager.' Suresh stopped drinking, stared at him and began laughing. He laughed till he was seized by a bout of loud coughing.

'I am better off, even if jobless. Office and administration manager! Bloody chutiya,' he snickered with contempt as Vinod grew red in the face.

'We have all been put in the soup by that chit of an accountant! He's the CEO of the company, can you imagine?' Vinod said, flashing the front page of a local newspaper that had a half page advertisement of Super Cabs. 'Have you seen this?'

'Advertisements all over the country, huh? The model is mast, huh? Venugopal must be sleeping with her…' a blurry-eyed Suresh said before downing his drink.

'She is that dork Hitesh's girlfriend. They live in an apartment in Jubilee Hills. Do you know that he gets paid twice of what I make? Bloody, after twenty-five years...'

'What are you saying? He's getting in the sack with this bird? And here I am: all my property is lost, ten years of earnings gone in a jiffy. Bloody dhokla-eating haraamkhor!' He angrily crumpled the newspaper and threw it on the floor.

'He's pulled Varun into his gang as well. Mehta, Varun and he are running these companies; they call all the shots! I hear Venugopal has lost it. He drinks all day and is openly having a dozen affairs with starlets. He recently ordered a Rolls Royce!'

Suresh responded with a bitter laugh. 'How's our friend Mohan Babu? He's been avoiding my calls, much like you did till recently.'

'I wasn't avoiding your calls, friend. Just that I had been really busy. Mohan's scared to death, and avoids me like plague. He's working night and day to meet production deadlines. The man has turned over a new leaf overnight. I have inside news that Venugopal is going to make him COO of the company.'

'Hmm...It's time for some action,' Suresh said, taking a swig from his mug of beer.

'But what can we do? I sold my apartment in Banjara Hills to pay back Venugopal Reddy. All that we earned over the last few years has been looted. I will have to stay in a rented apartment when we move to Hyderabad. But yes, we should indeed do something...' Vinod said, scratching his bald patch.

'Arey, stop nagging like a woman! Finish your drink and let me think,' Suresh said, annoyed, looking despicably around at the low-lifes that occupied the tables at the bar.

■

Enraged by Venugopal's action and the breach of his authority, Hitesh had half a mind to quit. He tried hard to suppress his growing frustration as he entered Venugopal's cabin. The latest addition to the office décor included various photographs of Venugopal, clicked alongside skimpily dressed actresses from the Telugu film industry, instead of the paintings that had previously hung on the same walls. Hitesh had heard from his colleagues that Venugopal now came to office only for a couple of hours in the afternoon and virtually lived in a five-star hotel where he had a suite booked in his name.

'Mr Hitesh, the CEO of Super Cabs! Come in,' Venugopal said in a hoarse voice as he saw Hitesh.

Hitesh smiled at him weakly and sat opposite him. 'How are you, sir?'

'I was fine till I received a call about one of your recent decisions. So you've decided to cancel the expansion of the Bangalore and Gurgaon licences, and take back the vehicles?' He walked across the room and poured himself a glass of Bombay Sapphire.

'Venu, we haven't been doing well in these cities; there's too much competition. The franchisees have been losing money and putting pressure on us. Besides, we are struggling to meet delivery commitments on vehicles to new franchisees, in what seems to be more promising markets in the North. The production team at Supreme Motors is unable to come to grips...'

'I've put them on a third shift this morning. Mr Mehta spoke to Mohan Babu. We have to meet sales targets for the company, Hitesh. I'm offloading my stake through a public offering, do you understand that?' Venugopal said in a raised voice.

Hitesh turned his gaze away from his bloodshot eyes. 'Yes, sir.'

'And you should support the franchisees to improve their business. Go and spend time in these centres personally; sign on agreements with software and BPO companies in these cities. It is okay if Super Cabs works at no profit here; these are high-profile markets nonetheless.' Venugopal paused for a moment and added, 'After all, you have spent fifteen per cent of your marketing budget in these two cities alone, having done high-profile launches!'

'Yes… We have,' Hitesh said, stung by the rebuke.

'Bring in a good marketing person from Heinz or Axis. I don't think the multiple shoots with your girlfriend are serving the company any purpose, if all you have to do is to shut down franchisees at the end of the day!'

Hitesh felt a knife pierce his heart. He knew a game had begun between him and the crooks, with Varun at the helm. 'I'm working night and day for this company, Venu. If you think I'm not meeting your expectations, then maybe I'm not the right person for this job…'

'Relax, Hitesh. I mean to say that there are some areas where you're doing really well, but you should consult others on all matters.'

'I understand,' Hitesh said, regaining his composure.

■

It was Friday. Hitesh shut his laptop and got up to leave for the day. Sushma hadn't returned from Mumbai, as promised. She hadn't taken most of his calls during the week. And sometimes when she had, she had cut the conversation short, citing that she was busy with a shoot.

He received a text message, hoping that it was from Sushma. It was; it said that she was moving in with a friend till she completed an assignment.

Annoyed, he dialled her number. She picked up after a few rings. 'Hi, how was your day? Did you go for any audition?' he asked calmly.

'Yes, I had a few meetings with producers. It's been a very busy day,' she said, sounding businesslike and distant.

'When are you coming back? I'm missing you. It's been a week.'

'Am I your babysitter? I've been working here, Hitesh. You made me quit, didn't you? Now that things are taking off, you want me to come and sit in your apartment…'

'Our apartment,' Hitesh corrected her. 'And relax. I just asked when you're heading back, Sush.'

'Whatever. I'm going to this party now and getting late. Bye.' She disconnected before Hitesh could say bye.

He walked out of his cabin, head hung low. He saw Payal at her desk, still working, while everyone else in the office had left. He checked the time; it was past nine.

'Why are you still here, Payal?'

'You didn't say I could leave, sir. I checked with you at seven. You asked me to wait then.'

'Oh God! I'm sorry!' Hitesh put his hand over his forehead. 'Isn't it your birthday today? Someone had brought a cake and told me; I meant to come out and wish you. I'm sorry. Happy birthday, Payal.'

'It's okay, sir. Thank you.'

'So do you have plans to go out with friends? Let me drop you wherever you need to be.'

'No, sir. It's just another day with my brother and father,' she said with a sad smile. 'I don't know too many people. We moved here three years ago when my father got transferred. He works for a bank.'

'Well, I must make up for making you sit so late in the office. Let's celebrate your birthday over dinner.'

'Sir, you don't have to...' she said, blushing.

'No, I insist. Moreover, both of us work very hard. It's okay for us to treat ourselves once in a while.'

'Okay. I'll just call home, sir.'

He punched the buttons on his phone and reserved a table for tea at the Taj Krishna. She walked ahead of him shyly, and he couldn't help but notice a beautiful smile on her face.

■

Hitesh ordered a second cup of coffee as he waited for Sushma. She had promised to meet him at Gloria Jean's at four, and it was past five already. He had cancelled a meeting with a journalist from a national newspaper to meet her. The journalist had wanted to do a story on Hitesh and his overwhelming tale of success. Hitesh had promised to meet him the following day.

His mind wandered to the increasing problems at Super Cabs. Hitesh and Varun had lately been through a series of arguments over the high-handedness and other questionable practices regarding recruitment of drivers, and their training by some of the franchisees in the North, and in Bangalore and Mysore. Customer complaints regarding rash driving and misbehaviour by the drivers were on a rise, and earnings had begun to dip. However the franchisees had Varun's steadfast support and were putting the blame on the quality and maintenance of the fleet, as well the marketing efforts at Super Cabs.

Suddenly, he saw Sushma walk in. She wore a black tube top paired with deep blue skinny jeans. Heads turned at the café; a lot of male attention was drawn in her direction. She sat opposite Hitesh after planting a quick peck on his cheek.

'You didn't have to come all the way to Mumbai. I've been so busy with shoots and meetings,' she said in a dull voice, while Hitesh ordered her a frappé.

'I had to see you, Sushma. It's been three weeks.'

'Ah, huh…I've been terribly busy.'

'Anyway, let's go to Red Light and party tonight. What do you say?'

'Not tonight, Hitesh. I've got to attend a fundraiser at Blue Frog. It's a paid assignment.' He noticed many changes in her appearance: her hair was curled and streaked brown.

'Well, it's okay. I've got tickets for Goa this weekend; bookings at the Hyatt.' He smiled at her, while she looked away and sipped on her frappé.

'I can't go. I'm shooting in Alibaug this weekend,' she replied, still looking away.

'Damn! Here goes another weekend! When do we spend time together, Sush? You're here; I'm in Hyderabad…' said an infuriated Hitesh.

'You didn't ask me before you planned Goa, did you?' Sushma retorted angrily. Seeing Hitesh's face change colour, she calmed down. She looked him straight in the eye and began, 'Good that you came here, Hitesh. I needed to talk to you. In fact, I was going to call you.' She paused as Hitesh stared at her, absolutely still. 'We have different priorities, Hitesh. I don't see myself as your wife. I have three-four years of good work left in me; this is what I always wanted to do and will do.' She averted his gaze and lowered her eyes. 'It's time we take a break from this thing we have. I've moved here, to Mumbai. I was in Hyderabad for a day last week, while you were in Bangalore…' she said carefully and bit her lower lip. He looked aghast, rage building up inside him, and pushed his cup of coffee away.

'Alright! Don't fucking look at me like that. You don't own me. It's good we're taking this break; we both can focus on our careers.'

Sushma stared at Hitesh's face, as if waiting for him to say something. He didn't. She grew restless and got up. 'I need to leave now. It's time for my dance class. We will get over it soon,' she said, picking up her disposable cup and moving towards the exit. Her phone buzzed. She picked it up and said, 'Yeah, come and pick me up.' 'Who was that?' Hitesh asked.

'Oh, it's Akhil, a fellow model and a friend… Anyway, we'll talk in a few weeks; I'll call you. We'll see where we are.' She ruffled his hair, kissed him on the cheek and walked out of the café without looking back. Hitesh watched her get on a motorbike behind a tall, slim guy wearing an Ed Hardy T-shirt, with a chiselled frame and a tattoo on his arm. She put her arms around him before they sped away, while Hitesh sat back, dumbfounded, cursing his luck.

CHAPTER 17

Sukanya knocked on the door and walked into Hitesh's cabin, tears rolling down her cheeks. He was glued to his laptop screen and didn't look up at her.

'Sir, I want to leave. I can't do this anymore...' she said and broke down.

'What happened, Sukanya?'

'Sir, the franchisees in Noida, Gurgaon, Bangalore and Mysore are proving to be very troublesome. They are apparently fronts for powerful politicians, and their goons are masquerading as cab drivers.'

'What are you saying?'

'We receive a number of complaints from many customers every day. People call up and say that they were treated badly by the drivers: their change wasn't returned, at times the drivers were drunk, and goons accompanied the drivers on trips and refused to get off and much more. There have been cases of eve-teasing in these cities. And now, in Noida, a case has been filed for attempt of rape!'

'What?' Hitesh stood up and began pacing the room.

'It happened last night. A woman took a cab from the airport and she was...' Sukanya hesitated a moment. 'She luckily had pepper spray and escaped.'

'Have you talked to Varun about this issue?'

Sukanya sighed and looked away. 'I have had many disagreements with him about the way these franchisees are functioning. When I spoke to him this morning about the latest issue, he hurled a volley of abuses at me and even threatened me,' she replied, shivering in her chair.

Hitesh was nonplussed. He called up Sanjay Thakur, the sole owner of those four franchisees.

'What is this I'm hearing, Sanjay? There is no discipline among your drivers!' a furious Hitesh said.

'It's a small matter and will be taken care of by the police. I have paid them already. The woman who has filed a case is a stupid bitch making unnecessary noise. She has no morals. She herself wore skimpy clothes and spoilt the mind of the poor driver.'

Hitesh was enraged. 'Let's not play games, Sanjay. We've been receiving a lot of complaints about your operations.'

'And what should I do? You have received your money, haven't you? How much more do you need to stay quiet?'

'Sanjay, you will promptly fire the accused driver! We are sending you a list of other drivers in a few minutes; they need to be straightened out.'

'Otherwise what will you do, hain?'

'The contract with your agency will be terminated. We have a number of other interested parties. In fact, I wonder how you won the bid in the first place,' Hitesh hollered, immediately regretting his last words.

'We will fire a few drivers and warn the rest, hain? Theek hai ji? Let's not have problems. You and we are partners, right?' Sanjay's tone changed.

'We want to see prompt corrective action. We will issue a press release and apology to that effect.'

'Theek hai,' Sanjay said lamely before hanging up.

'What did you just do? You warned a franchise owner, didn't you? How could you?' Hitesh heard Varun bark, storming into the cabin. Varun glared angrily at Sukanya, who was sipping some water.

An irate Hitesh got up and walked towards him. 'How dare you question me like that? Now get out of my office; I don't want to deal with you.'

'What will you do if I don't?' Varun stood defiant. A crowd gathered outside the cabin.

'I will hand over my resignation to the board. It's either you or me. Let them make the choice.'

The expression on Varun's face changed all of a sudden. 'Relax. You're taking this too seriously. I didn't mean to challenge you...' Varun pleaded, knowing that he had crossed the line, and had overplayed his hand.

'Sure, Varun. Now please leave. You've created a scene already. Be prepared to answer the board on charges of harassing and abusing a woman employee.'

Varun opened his mouth to say something but stopped. He threw an angry glance at Sukanya, and stormed out of the cabin.

All the attempts by Mehta and Venugopal Reddy over the next week, to broker peace between Varun and Hitesh failed; Hitesh did not relent. All the franchisees they had planned on were on board. It was decided that Varun had more nuisance value than Hitesh, and had outlived his usefulness. So he was, reluctantly, let go on health grounds by the end of the week. Hitesh noticed his quiet exit. He was told that G. S. Rao had called in Varun for a chat, and assumed that he had been warned with dire consequences if he made any trouble for the company.

It had been six weeks since the fateful day when he went to Mumbai to pay a surprise visit to Sushma. Initially, he waited for her calls all day and hoped she would return to Hyderabad. She never called him, and mostly ignored his calls. Sometimes when she did answer, she hung up after talking for a minute or two. Hitesh spent his evenings pining for her and remembering their moments together. Sometimes, he woke up in the middle of the night and wept. Soon, he began to stay up most of the night, longing for her.

Sleep-deprived and overworked, he became increasingly irritable at work. There had been many instances where he was unnecessarily rude or blew his top off on staff and on a couple of franchisees. He wondered where his life was going. He had a stressful job, and his life outside office was a question mark. He began spending his weekends with his parents and, occasionally, his friends, who were busy running their own rat race.

■

Hitesh was in his cabin, staring at the monitor, unable to concentrate on his work. Last evening after office, he had called up Sushma again. She had snapped at him for calling her late. Hitesh had then run his car into a divider, driving back home at manic speed.

Now, he picked up his phone and dialled her number. 'Yes, how can I help you?' a woman asked in a raspy voice.

'I want to speak to Sushma, please,' he quipped.

'She can't come on the phone; she's doing her hair for a shoot.'

'Tell her it's Hitesh on the line.'

'Who is it?' he heard Sushma yell in the background.

'Some Hitesh insists he must talk to you.'

'Oh, tell him I can't.'

'Who is he?' a guy's voice came.

'He is a client; got me the Super Cabs gig. He pesters me no end, calling all the time,' Sushma said with irritation. Hitesh heard muffled laughter, and a guy mumble a cuss word meant for him. The line went dead.

He picked himself up and nodded his head, before he covered his face with his palms. He grew bitter and cursed himself for being miserable about a woman who had used him, and then thrown him out of her life like a used tissue.

He decided to leave office early, and picked up his bag to leave. It was past six.

He opened the glass door to see Payal and the rest of the staff standing outside his door, a wide grin on their faces. Payal held a chocolate cake in her hands, and the whole group entered his cabin screaming 'SURPRISE'.

It was his birthday and he had completely forgotten about it. He had cut his mother's call twice in the morning, and was yet to call her back. The whole team hummed along as Payal sang 'Happy birthday, dear Hitesh,' and even force-fed him a piece of cake.

He thanked everyone, and they all left. Payal stayed back to clear up. 'Thank you,' he said to her.

'We aren't done yet,' she said, smiling and looking at him mischievously.

'We aren't?' Hitesh asked, sounding dull and tired.

'I've booked a table for both of us at Our Place for dinner,' she chirped. Then, in an animated voice, she continued, 'Both of us work very hard. It's okay to treat ourselves once in a while.' She grinned and looked into his eyes. Hitesh didn't respond for a while and stared at her. He noticed that Payal had made an effort to dress up that day, a change from her usually demure self. She was wearing a white churidar with a lime-green kurta, and had a small bindi on her forehead. She looked pretty, earrings tinkling as she laughed. The attention she had been showering on him for a while now hadn't escaped his eyes, only he had been too busy and stressed out to bother. 'Why are you doing this, Payal? I hope you realize that I'm your boss and you're an employee.' Hitesh asked, keeping a straight face.

Payal flinched; Hitesh had never been so rude to her before. 'That doesn't matter, Hitesh. The reason why I am doing this is because I care for you, just like you care for everybody. I know that deep down, beneath all the shouting you've been doing lately, you're a good person at heart. And please don't think that all those who come close to you have ulterior motives.' Hitesh recoiled, as if Payal had read his mind. But what she had just said were the nicest things he had heard about himself in a long time.

'Let's leave. I'm sick of this damned office,' he said, managing a smile. 'Shall we drop by my home for a few minutes so I meet my parents?' She smiled a yes.

CHAPTER 18

Hitesh woke up to the shrill ringing of the phone. He saw the time; it was past eleven. 'Hello,' he said in a sleepy voice.

'We have a bit of a problem,' Mehta wheezed at the other end.

'What happened?'

'Do you get the *Andhra Observer*? It's a local paper.'

'No, I don't... But what's wrong? Is there something about Super Cabs?'

'There's a half-page piece by the paper claiming that a murder took place at our manufacturing facility a year ago, and that the management had hushed it up then, calling it a suicide. It's an explosive piece, the worst news we could get on a Sunday morning. There are pictures of the deceased young man and quotes by his family, demanding justice.'

'Who exactly is said to be responsible? Does it mention any names?' a worried Hitesh asked.

'Mohan Babu has been indicated as the murderer. We all know about this, don't we? His name is mentioned thrice in the story, and that he had threatened and warned the young worker many times, in the presence of his family. Venugopal's phone hasn't stopped ringing since morning. Reach his place in thirty minutes. He wants to see both of us.'

Hitesh dressed up hurriedly and was outside Venugopal's villa, after a short drive, when he received a call from a prominent journalist in the state. Hitesh feigned ignorance of the news and claimed that he knew nothing about the facts of the case, before abruptly ending the call. He realized that a controversy such as this could spell doom for Super Cabs, given the close alignment with Supreme Motors.

He entered the bungalow to see a furious-looking Venugopal, barking instructions to one of his minions. Mehta sat quietly in a corner, his face bearing a nervous frown.

'What do we do now, Hitesh? There will be bloodbath in the stock exchange...' Venu spat out.

'I'm sure this is a conspiracy by one of G.S. Rao's political rivals,' Mehta blurted out.

'What is G.S. Rao saying?' Hitesh asked.

'He hasn't given any statement till now. He has escaped to his farmhouse near Bangalore, and is likely to return only after a week,' Venugopal said.

'How has Mohan Babu taken it?'

'He called up at eight and pleaded innocence; he is very scared,' Mehta said.

'What can be done? Such a mess I've been put into by that fellow,' Venugopal said bitterly, looking tensed and scratching his unshaven chin.

'This needs careful handling, sir. Mohan Babu is responsible smooth production to meet delivery deadlines. He needs to be managed tactfully. We have been under fire since Varun Rao's departure, thanks to a number of difficult franchisees with questionable backgrounds,' Hitesh said as Venugopal listened with rapt attention.

'We should ask him to resign till the case is solved...' Mr Mehta suggested meekly. He clearly had no love lost for Mohan Babu, who had had him assaulted by retrenched employees a few years ago.

'But is the case going to be reopened? It's just an opinion piece in a local newspaper,' Hitesh ventured, while Venugopal held his head, looking confused.

Venugopal's phone rang and he walked out of the room to take the call in his balcony. He came back looking relieved.

'It was G.S. Rao Garu. He suggests that we should ask Mohan Babu to resign, and pay him on the side to make up for the lost salary. We should pay him five years' salary as compensation, and let him retire voluntarily. The company should release a statement that the case is personal, between Mohan Babu and the deceased's family; the company had nothing to do with the conflict; and we expect and hope that justice is delivered.'

'This could work,' Mr Mehta said with a wry smile.

'But will Mohan Babu leave the company quietly?' Hitesh expressed his concern, looking unconvinced and disturbed by the suggestion. He knew Mohan to be a slippery and vile strongman, who could swoop down to any level to protect his own interests.

'He will,' Venugopal retorted. 'Rao Garu will call him, promising support to close the case, and to assure that nothing would happen to him. He will also promise him to give party work, and a possible seat for the coming election. It can be positioned as a decision to leave in order to serve the people. The article can be defended, saying that this is a conspiracy by the opposition.'

'Yes Venu, you are right. Better to get him out of the way before things get worse. He is a dangerous man and, given his association with the company, his actions can leave us with a black mark. I can see that our share prices would be affected by this piece of news,' Mehta said, sounding like the apostle of impending gloom.

'The stupid gangster! I'll call him right away,' Venugopal hollered as he scrolled through his address book, sweat forming on his brows, and it seemed that his blood pressure was on the rise.

CHAPTER 19

'Come, come Mohan Babu. So you've finally got time to meet your old friends,' G.V. Vinod said with a wicked smile, as a bewildered Mohan Babu, dressed in a crumpled white kurta, his paunch sticking out, staggered towards them in the dimly lit bar.

'Nice picture in today's paper, isn't it? This one was taken during the company trip to Ooty five years ago, isn't it? You were thinner, and had more hair on your head then,' Suresh grinned as he puffed on his Charminar, as Mohan Babu moved into the seat opposite them after a bit of struggle.

'Shut up!' Mohan Babu barked. He picked up Suresh's mug of beer and flung it across the room. A waiter ran in quickly to clear up the mess.

'Relax, Mohan Babu. We are all friends,' a worried Vinod said. Suresh looked nonchalant and averted his gaze.

'Go and look at yourself in the mirror! You don't have money to buy a decent pack of cigarettes. You sit here every day like crows sit by the dustbin outside my house. And you dare to laugh at me?' Mohan hollered at Suresh. He then gestured to the waiter to bring him a bottle of whisky. The three smoked in silence, trying to dispel the visible tension in the air, in vain.

'Venugopal and G.S. Rao called me up a while back. Venu wants me to take voluntary retirement from the company, suggesting I focus on community work and get into politics full time. Rao Garu offered me his support and is giving me party work,' Mohan Babu finally broke the gloomy silence. He looked at the other two as if seeking a reaction, and quickly gulped down the whisky—neat.

'But you were up for a promotion, Mohan Garu,' Vinod said, showing him an email from Venugopal Reddy, that mentioned his promotion and increase of salary.

'Who do you think got this article put in a newspaper? It seems very convenient to retire you, and draft you into party work,' Suresh asked Mohan Babu, surreptitiously gesturing to Vinod to support him.

'Yes, very convenient indeed! Who can benefit from your exit?' Vinod added, pretending to think hard.

'Do you mean Super Cabs? Why will they print such news about me? Are they mad? I have been working like a maniac, meeting all their unrealistic production deadlines. This article will affect their share prices. Tch.' Mohan Babu barked and shook his head and then added, 'This must be a political conspiracy...'

'Is it? Then how do you explain what happened to me? Vinod is being moved to Hyderabad, and they plan to get him to retire soon. Varun Rao has been thrown out, and I hear he's in Dubai these days, managing some small business owned by G.S. Rao. All this has been a result of a strategic plan. It hasn't happened just like that,' Suresh said, gesticulating wildly and puffing away.

'Try to put things into context, Mohan Babu! There are people who will benefit from our dismissal, and it will serve their interests. Who do you think it is?' Vinod asked with feigned anxiety on his face.

'That fellow, Mehta! I will crush him the next time he comes to Vizag. He will not go back,' Mohan Babu growled as a satisfied smile appeared on Suresh's face.

'That old Mehta doesn't have the guts; he's just a foot soldier. Everything that's happened to us has been led by Venugopal Reddy, and that chit of a fellow, his accountant, Hitesh. Who do you think gathered all the evidence against our activities?' Suresh leaned in and poured himself a glass of whisky, while Vinod munched on peanuts.

'No, no, Suresh. You are speculating too much. This is Venugopal's company; why will he conspire to spoil its name? Moreover, he sounded much concerned about this situation. Also, he's kept his promise with me...'

'Listen, Mohan Garu, and listen carefully. I wasn't needed anymore and was dispensed with, immediately. Vinod was retained for six months because he deals with labour. Slowly, Mehta's people have infiltrated his ranks, and now he's a pariah. Varun was taken to be second-in-command for Venugopal's company. Eight months after he'd set up the entire business, he was fired and threatened and warned by G.S. Rao. Now, two weeks ago, Venugopal sold nearly his entire stake in Supreme Motors. In three months, he will step down, putting Mehta in charge to run it. He doesn't care anymore. He used you when he needed you; now you are useless for him. This Super Cabs is nothing but a scam for him to raise the share prices of Supreme Motors, and sell out. It's his conspiracy with those rats, Mehta and Hitesh. These fellows are getting a cut,' Suresh said, looking straight into Mohan Babu's stupefied eyes.

'Yes, Mohan Garu. This is a big conspiracy against you. They want to fix you. The plan was to fix all of us,' Vinod said emphatically.

'And you're the tallest figure among us. Venugopal gets all his ideas from that dirt bag, Hitesh. Did you know that the girl on all the Super Cabs hoardings is his girlfriend? Now the axe hangs on your head, Mohan Garu. It is the policy of divide and rule,' Suresh sniggered as Mohan Babu looked outraged.

'What you are speaking is true. I hear this Hitesh told someone that Mohan Babu's right place is behind bars. He calls you a thug and a gunda, and what not,' Vinod said, shaking his head in contempt. Mohan Babu slammed his fist on the table.

'Once you leave the company, they'll make sure you get arrested. Once you're tainted with a criminal charge, G.S. Rao will not give you a party ticket. Master stroke,' Suresh said, finishing his drink.

'I will break that bastard Hitesh's neck, and throw him into the sea,' Mohan barked.

'No, no, Mohan Babu. No violence,' Vinod screeched.

'I will get him picked up right now,' he said angrily, and picked up his phone to dial a number.

'Are you a fool? He's not just some accountant anymore; he's the CEO of Super Cabs. The national media will create a ruckus. I told you to knock him off when he was a plain auditor, but you didn't listen to me then. Now you'll do no such thing. Listen to me carefully. We have limited time. I have a plan to save you, and to teach that bastard a lesson,' Suresh said forcefully as Mohan Babu meekly put his phone down.

■

Vinod entered the small, cramped living room of the tiny apartment Suresh lived in. The furniture was sparse: two rickety chairs and a rugged cot. The wall cabinets were stuffed with much more than they could hold. The children, who were sitting and studying on the faded carpet got up and went inside as they saw Vinod enter. Suresh's docile wife brought him a glass of water. She kept her eyes on the floor as he gulped it.

Suresh walked in from outside, holding a black polythene bag in one hand and a bag of groceries in the other. The black bag seemed to hold a bottle of country liquor.

'What's the news about Mohan? Is he all geared up?' Suresh asked with authority as soon as he saw Vinod.

'I am coming from his house. He is ready to swing into action. I've also got some of my loyalists to muster support for him,' Vinod replied.

'Very good,' Suresh beamed, running his palm over his three-day-old stubble. 'I paid the reporter today. He did a very good job indeed, rekindling the old fires. I asked him to disappear for a few weeks. Are you ready?'

'Hmm…I don't know. Does it have to be me? I'm worried.'

'Of course it has to be you! That way, it will be more authentic. That Hitesh and Venugopal think that only they can plan and scheme, is it? I too can, better than they ever could.'

'I hope everything goes well,' Vinod said nervously.

'It will, I've got a lot of documents fed in from Varun about Super Cabs, which prove that Venugopal has been at the helm of affairs. I'm going to pass all that to friendly journalists, through informers here and in Hyderabad.'

'Very good,' Vinod said, relieved, taking out a pack of Gold Flakes and offering it to Suresh.

'I need Rs 20,000 for important expenses, Vinod. The journalists have to be paid,' Suresh said with a careful smile as Vinod scanned his eyes across the gloom and decay around him. His old friend was broke, and desperate to redeem himself.

'What's your benefit in this? Why are you doing this?'

'Just settling accounts,' Suresh replied gruffly, lighting up his cigarette and breaking into a wicked laugh.

CHAPTER 20

Hitesh had called his team to the meeting room, to inform them of the planned PR exercise for the next few days, given the decision of Mohan Babu to leave Supreme Motors. He instructed his key staff to call all the franchisees and to assure them of full support without disruption. His phone buzzed, but he ignored it. Payal barged into the room.

'Sorry, Hitesh; Mr Reddy is on line one. He wants to talk to you urgently,' she said, looking nervous. He followed her out of the room and took the call in his cabin.

'Disaster! Come over right away,' Venugopal said before hanging up. Thirty minutes later, Hitesh sat on the edge of his seat, watching the breaking news on the huge plasma screen in Venugopal Reddy's office. Mehta looked scared, and G.S. Rao looked ready to smash the screen.

IBS 360—Breaking News

In Vizag, workers at the Supreme Motors plant, in support of the agitation led by the company's production manager, Mohan Babu, have gone on an indefinite strike, stating the gross injustice meted out to the employees. Babu alleges that the company has cut staff and pay with the aim to survive and, in turn, has been selling vehicles at a small margin above costs to Super Cabs, which happens to be a front for the promoter group and various political interests. It is alleged that workers' interests have been compromised in order to make profits through the rental service owned by Mr Reddy and a prominent politician, and this whole plot is single-handedly run by a small-time accountant, Hitesh Patel. The manufacturing facility is now under lockdown, and all work has been stopped, the workers' representative says.

'There will be no negotiation in Hyderabad. I request Mr Reddy to come and listen to his workers in Vizag. They have been cheated in order to fill his coffers,' Mohan Babu said in a rehearsed tone, staring into the camera.

News 7*24

Mohan Babu refutes all allegations of murdering a fellow worker, alleging instead that this is a conspiracy by the management, and the political interests behind the chairman, Mr Reddy. He has said that the workers will not give in to the unrealistic demands and work at low salaries, while huge profits are being hoarded by Mr Reddy's car rental company, run by his acolyte, a young accountant, Hitesh Patel.

K News

Mohan Babu has provided documents that reveal some startling facts. Employees who were laid off by Supreme Motors have been hired back in the same company as temporary labour with no benefits, and made to work long hours while denying them overtime. Mohan Babu says that the workers are angry at the gross injustice that has been meted out to them.

Meanwhile, franchises of Super Cabs in Hyderabad, Nagpur and Indore, have denied knowing anything about Mr Reddy's interests in the company, and said that they are shocked with the recent developments. They are evaluating their future options and association with the company, some of them say.

Venugopal Reddy looked furious and paced the length of the room, while G.S. Rao, panic written all over his face, got up and rushed out of the cabin. Minutes later, OB vans stood outside the office building, and reporters and cameramen fought with the security to be led in. Payal called up Hitesh, saying that a couple of reporters had barged into the office, and were asking executives about the association with Supreme Motors. Hitesh advised her to call the police, and turned to look at Mehta who looked pale as death.

'I will go to Vizag and negotiate with him. Mr Mehta, call him up. This nonsense has to stop!' Venugopal screamed. He switched the channel to SNB Business, which showed that the share price of Supreme Motors was in a freefall. The analysts discussed how the shares had plunged by twenty per cent of the opening price, since morning. The verdict was to sell, given that the company would be unable to meet its delivery schedule to franchisees of Super Cabs; some of those were considering opting out of the business, given that maintenance schedules were unlikely to be met, because of the lack of servicing support.

Hitesh called up a few journalists he knew personally, and asked them to give the company a little more time to respond. However, he quickly understood that the situation had slipped out of control.

Mehta stared at the television screen blankly. His usual neatly combed mop of grey hair was dishevelled, and he had loosened his tie and taken off his blazer. Mohan Babu was not responding to his calls or messages. Hitesh had been receiving calls from angry franchisees; some of them mouthed profanities, and even threatened legal action if deliveries of the fleet, on which they had promised lease commitments, failed. Glum-faced, he turned on the plasma television in the conference room.

IBS 360

There has been no word from the management at Supreme Motors and Super Cabs, who appear to be huddled into a discussion at the Supreme Motors' office in Vizag. Workers are chanting slogans claiming exploitation, fraud and harassment. They are demanding the immediate ouster of Hitesh Patel, Mehta and Venugopal Reddy from the management. They also want the government to investigate into the affairs of the company. One worker, Rajshekar, attempted self-immolation, and was rescued by fellow workers. Meanwhile, employees are burning effigies of Hitesh Patel and Venugopal Reddy, and it appears that the opposition party mobs have joined the protests that have taken a violent turn.

News 7*24

We have just heard from our correspondent that Mr G.V. Vinod, 56, HR manager of Supreme Motors, who came to meet the protesters a while back in an attempt to calm the situation, was struck by stones and chappals, and ended up being beaten with a hockey stick by an angry worker. A bruised Mr Vinod was taken to a nearby hospital, and is said to be stable. Mohan Babu has apologized to Mr Vinod, and has requested the workers to continue a peaceful protest.

K News

In the latest incident, two cabs run by the Super Cabs franchisee in Vizag were stopped by angry mobs, and were set afire. There have been no casualties, and the drivers are reported to have fled from the scene, after being pushed around by the irate mobs. Our correspondent has received documents that clearly manifest the relationship between Supreme Motors and Super Cabs. We have received transcripts of the meetings, bank statements and the shocking finding that Mr Mehta, the CFO of Supreme Motors, was actively involved in decision-making at Super Cabs. Three franchisees who we spoke to, said that they plan to sue Super Cabs for misrepresentation and fraud, as well as terminate their relationship with them. Meanwhile, Mr Venugopal Reddy's effigies are being given the same treatment in Hyderabad as in Vizag. Mr Reddy is known to be a small-time film producer and, according to sources, is often spotted in parties and has strong political connections…

Venugopal flung the remote and then a vase of flowers at the television screen, rudely shocking Hitesh, who was frantically working over the phone to persuade franchisees not to talk to the media, or take any radical decisions. G.S. Rao called up Venugopal to tell him that he had been summoned to meet the chief minister, who was under growing political pressure from the opposition and the central government, to investigate the matter. He was told that the stock exchange had suspended the trading of Supreme Motors shares that had plunged to Rs 30. The investors were screaming bloodbath, and the sentiment was down; the index had closed at 150 basis points lower.

'Mehta, go downstairs and talk to the media. Tell them that things will be under control. Accept that Supreme Motors is one of the promoters and investors in Super Cabs, but insist that it's run independently. Tell them that negotiations are underway,' a much-stressed-out Venugopal instructed Mehta who looked spooked. He appeared more willing to jump from the window, than to go down to meet the media, who had herded on the street outside the office, demanding an explanation.

'Hitesh, you too go down and tell them about the good job you've done. Promise corrective action, and assure your franchisees that things will be okay. I need to go and meet some people,' Venugopal said, before he made a call, and barked instructions to his driver to bring a car near the emergency exit.

A reluctant Hitesh went down with a deadpan Mehta behind him. They opened the door but were blinded by the flashbulbs that went off immediately. Microphones were thrust into their faces, and furious questioning, sledging and allegations began. The two stood flabbergasted before an angry media, who had been waiting under the blistering April sun since morning.

CHAPTER 21

Day 2

Hitesh entered the office with Payal in tow. She had stayed up with him almost throughout the previous night, helping him to put together responses to the media and field questions from angry franchisees.

They hadn't heard from Mehta or Venugopal the last evening; both of them were reeling under tremendous pressure from the media.

He frowned when he saw the front-page news in *AP Times*: 'Lockdown at Supreme Motors, Allegations of Exploitation and Fraud'.

He scanned through the business papers. 'Supreme Motors Puts a Brake on the Bull Run'; 'Another Scam, Another Bloodbath'; 'Supreme Motors Stock Plunges by 80%'.

Hitesh sat on a chair and covered his face with his palms. It was much more than he could handle. The break-up with Sushma had hurt him enough, but he had coped with it. But how was he to handle the shame and embarrassment of being labelled a fraud? How would he answer the investors, and those employees who lost their jobs overnight? Would his own career get ruined just after its take-off? The previous night, his mother had called him up in panic, saying that his father's blood pressure had shot up and he had to be rushed to the hospital by the neighbours. The reporters had showed up at his home, asking questions about his integrity.

He looked up to see the staff walk in. They seemed low in spirits, eyes hovering around his glass cabin, as if seeking instructions on how to handle the crisis. A few had called in sick, feigning illness to avoid getting badgered by the reporters and franchisees, who had now progressed to shouting and abusing, given the bad press.

Hitesh got off the phone with the franchisees in Nashik and Ranchi, who had decided to jump off the sinking ship. He was unable to persuade them to do otherwise.

'This is going to be breaking news now,' he said worriedly to his team of managers. Payal, glum-faced, took down notes.

'What do we do?' Sukanya asked.

'We can't do much; we've been pushed into a corner. All franchisees have paid us for a lease on a fleet of fifty vehicles. We've delivered twenty to twenty-five, and, on the remaining, we await deliveries. All the funds we've received have either been remitted to Supreme Motors, or been used up in advertising, PR and customer support. We have only two months, worth of cash to pay salaries, and to meet expenses. I believe that the franchisees will hold back remittance of our share of their revenues, as we won't be able to meet delivery obligations. We can only ask for a partial return of funds from Supreme Motors...'

'Hitesh, my father has messaged to turn on the news channel,' Payal interrupted.

Hitesh turned on the television and watched the screen in dismay.

SNB Business

Stock trading of Supreme Motors has been suspended till further notice. SEBI will investigate into the ownership of Super Cabs, and the divesting of company stock by the promoter, Mr Reddy.

The company is likely to be delisted from the stock exchange. Investors are crying foul, and have raised a furor. Certain trading houses are also being monitored to investigate fraud and allegations of insider trading.

IBS 360

Protests continue today outside the Supreme Motors plant. The company had promised negotiation, but Mohan Babu claims that Mr Reddy is yet to contact him.The Chief Minister, Mr B.K. Reddy, visited the plant this morning and sympathized with the workers, requesting them to call off their strike. It's unclear what their demands are, apart from the removal of Mr Venu Reddy and his trusted executives from the management. The opposition leader Mr Ranga Naidu expressed his solidarity with the workers, and has demanded a CBI probe into the workings of the company.

News 7*24

It is reported that Venu Reddy is not in Hyderabad, and has left the city in a private jet. His current whereabouts are unknown. Meanwhile, the Vizag franchisee has stopped operating its vehicles in the city over fears of being attacked. It is reported that this franchise is owned by R.D. Rao, the son in-law of State Education Minister G.S. Rao. Many hoardings featuring the company's advertisements have been pulled down and, in some cases, have been painted black. The HR Manager G.V. Vinod is reported to be stable and recovering. His family claims that he has been under tremendous strain over the past few months, as Mr Venu Reddy put growing pressure on workers to meet strict delivery deadlines, under difficult working conditions.

K News

Breaking News: State Education Minister, G.S. Rao, handed in his resignation a few minutes ago citing health concerns. He was involved in negotiations with the chief minister, and members of the central ruling party, who want to continue the alliance with his faction that provides the government the much-needed numbers to form a majority. The opposition, meanwhile, is making an all out bid to woo as many as fifteen of his twenty-one MLAs, which would put them back in the saddle, and in a position to prove their majority. G.S. Rao's arch rival Ranga Naidu said that G.S. Rao's actions are shameful. It pains him to see how poor workers have been exploited and looted for a few well-heeled thugs, to make more money. He demands a strict investigation into this scam. The workers deserve justice.

Opposition party workers are outside G.S. Rao's home in Jubilee Hills, burning tyres, and chanting slogans. The opposition party MLAs also staged a walk out from the assembly, a few moments ago.

Hitesh saw Mehta enter the office and walk towards the meeting room. He looked gutted and in haste.

Hitesh followed him inside. 'Hitesh, Venu Reddy has left the country. He tendered his resignation to the Board, and passed a resolution to make me the acting CEO of Supreme Motors. I think he's left for Switzerland or Canada. His family is at the airport too.' Hitesh sat down slowly, trying to digest the news; the others in the room grew irate, and mumbled their disapproval of Venu's action. He was pondering hard about what to do when he received a text message from Sahil. 'A lot of people are asking questions: SEBI, police, ministers, company affairs, CPA board, media. partner pissed off. What the hell have you done? You're in deep shit, boss!' Hitesh's heart skipped a beat, as he read and reread the message.

Just then, he received a call from the Delhi franchisee. Mehta, meanwhile, was trying to refute Venu Reddy's whereabouts to a reporter on phone. 'Boss, deliver the vehicles or return the money. Three days! Otherwise, you will be shot, samjha kya?' Hitesh hung up as if coming out of a trance, and saw Mehta pleading with the reporter not to reveal that Venu Reddy had left the country.

CHAPTER 22

Hitesh seemed to have aged over ten years in the last four days; unkempt hair, sunken eyes, a perpetual baffled expression on the face. He had never had many friends, but on this day he felt lonely, very lonely. He wished he could pour his heart out to someone, someone who would just listen to him, and not make him stand in a box, awaiting judgment. He longed for Sushma, and became even more bitter. He tried to brush her thoughts aside, and focus on the problem at hand. He wondered if he should run away; after all, he knew that the investigation into the scam wouldn't leave him unblemished. But he knew he couldn't, though he was losing the will to fight, he had to stand up, for himself and for the staff who depended on him.

It was almost nine and he was still in office. The staff had left for the day. He envied them their simple existence; all they could lose in the storm was a job at Super Cabs. Hitesh, on the other hand, stood to lose everything: his career, respect in the society and the trust of those who cared for him. He remembered his days at Smith & Donald; the problems he faced then now seemed trivial.

He saw someone open his cabin door. Hitesh was surprised to see it was Payal. What was she doing so late in the office? Had he again asked her to wait, and forgotten all about it? He opened his mouth to ask but stopped as she quietly came inside and sat beside him on the table. 'Hitesh, I do not know what you'll make of it, but I just couldn't leave you in this state and go home,' she began. Hitesh turned his face away. 'I have an idea of what has been going on in the company for the last few months. Having worked with Supreme Motors, I always knew that Venugopal, Mohan Babu and even Vinod and Varun, are people one should keep a safe distance from,' she said, pausing to see if Hitesh was listening. He was quiet; his head hung low. 'All I want to say is that you can count on me for any help you may want.' Hitesh looked up and was about to say he didn't need any, when he stopped. Her face looked so innocent; her eyes behind the frames were devoid of any false intention. 'And yes, I do not expect anything as you might think,' she added, and rose to leave. Hitesh held her hand, and motioned her to sit. She did; the two sat in silence for a while. Hitesh felt her presence comforting. Payal liked him, he knew that. Why, he never came to know. He was no more the successful CEO of a booming company, but a fallen man, detested by many and labelled a cheat. Hitesh realized that his failed relationship with Sushma had made him cynical. Payal wasn't asking him for anything in return.

'Thank you, Payal,' he said.

Her eyes lit up and lips stretched into a pleasant smile. 'It is a bad phase, but it will pass soon, so let's not kill ourselves over it. Nothing is so bad in the world as to stop you from enjoying all that you still have,' she chirped. 'In fact, I have a plan to…' she added when Hitesh interrupted her. 'The dinner on my birthday was the first time I saw you like this, Payal: all chirpy and happy. If I may ask, why are you so serious all the time? You don't seem to mix with people easily.'

She suddenly became silent. Then, slowly, she spoke, 'You're right, Hitesh. Few people know me like this. For most, I am this dull and boring person who would answer every offer of friendship with a scowl. But I find myself just incapable of trusting anybody.' She became silent again.

'Why, Payal? Had a bad relationship in the past?'

'No, Hitesh. Actually, I don't even remember when I turned like this. Maybe, after my mother's death…' She stopped, choked.

'I'm so sorry, Payal. I remember you once told me that you would celebrate your birthday with your brother and father. I didn't ask you then.'

'Let's talk about this some other time. Now you must listen to my plan. You are coming to my house for dinner. My brother and father will be pleased to have you there. It's 9.30 already. So let's not waste any more time,' she said and smiled.

'Dinner at your house? Oh, no, no. We can go to some restaurant...'

'My place it will be. You are coming, that's it. Or should I take back my generous offer of lending you a shoulder to cry on?' she grinned.

Hitesh laughed. He realized that he hadn't laughed like this since a long time. 'Okay, as you say, ma'am,' he replied, taking his office bag, looking much relaxed.

The small, two-bedroom flat was a twenty-five-minute drive from office. Payal had called home, while in the car, to inform her father that Hitesh would be coming. Both her father and brother greeted them at the door. Hitesh greeted them back and, hesitantly, entered the house. He noticed that the walls were mostly bare, other than a framed, garlanded photograph of a middle-aged woman. Hitesh knew it was Payal's mother from the stark resemblance between their faces. Her mother was beautiful.

Payal's father and brother made Hitesh comfortable, while she retired to the kitchen. About half an hour later, they all sat down for dinner.

Hitesh was quite at ease by now. Payal's father was a jovial man who liked to crack jokes and make everyone laugh. He even mentioned his late wife twice or thrice in the conversation, talking smilingly about her as if she weren't dead at all. Hitesh liked him for being so lively, despite the tragedy. He discussed with Hitesh the scam and the allegations, and seemed concerned for him. Payal's brother, two years older than her, was a simple, serious-looking guy who seemed to be very protective about his sister. Hitesh liked the way the family talked to each other at the dinner table, narrating events of the day and giving each other suggestions and advice. He thought of his own family and the way they used to have dinner together. They would eat quietly, the silence broken now and then by his mother's grumblings or father's sarcastic comments about his job and salary. General discontent ran in his family's blood, he thought.

Hitesh had eaten heartily after many days. As he got up to wash his hands, his phone rang. It was Rajesh, his friend from school. Anxious, Hitesh picked it up. 'Hitesh, where are you? Good you haven't reached your apartment yet. I went there to see you after watching the news, and found your place swarming with reporters. They are all waiting for you, to jump on you with questions. It's quite a scene here. Wherever you are, don't go to your place tonight. See if you can stay elsewhere. Sorry yaar, I wish you could stay at my place but…but my father… Hope you understand.'

'I do, Rajesh. Thank you for informing me. You did me a great favour.'

'Bye, yaar. Do call me if you need any other help.'

'Sure, Rajesh,' Hitesh replied and disconnected. He looked forlorn again.

He turned around to see three anxious faces looking at him. He told them about the problem at hand, at which they looked at one another as if reaching a silent agreement. 'You are staying here tonight,' Payal said in a tone of finality.

'Yes, you can if you like,' her father added.

Hitesh was hesitant initially, but gave in as they all insisted. Moreover, he could not think of anywhere else to go.

His bed was arranged in her brother's room, her brother's in the main hall.

As her father went to bed, she asked him if he could take Hitesh to show the terrace. He nodded and they both went upstairs.

A cool breeze touched their faces, causing them to relax and forget office for some time. 'You are lucky to have such a nice family, Payal,' Hitesh said. Payal smiled, but suddenly became serious. 'It is nothing to what it used to be when my mother was alive. We were one happy bunch. Behind all that laughter, my father really yearns for my mother. It has been three years now since that fateful accident. We lived in Surat then. After her death, my father could not live in the same house anymore. He applied for a transfer, and we all came to Hyderabad,' she said, with faraway eyes.

'Do you have friends here?'

'No, not many. In fact, nobody,' she smirked. 'I do keep in touch with my old friends from college though. It's difficult for me to make new relationships.'

'But you can't cling to the old ones all your life. Give yourself another chance; who knows, you might find friends who would become closer to you than the old ones...' Hitesh stopped, realizing how little he believed in his own philosophy.

'You are right,' she said thoughtfully. 'Tell me, Hitesh, what do you want from your life?'

He became silent. The question seemed to hit his mind like a stone hitting still water. What did he want from life? He realized he had never been very ambitious, but had always wanted a life better than that of his parents'. He wanted to earn well and, lead a comfortable life in which he would not be denied the luxuries of the rich. He wanted a loving wife, who believed in him and had enough time for him. It struck him that most of his life was spent in satisfying his parents' dreams and, the past few months, in living up to Sushma's expectations, instead of his own needs. 'I don't know,' he finally said. 'What do you want, Payal?'

'Well,' she hesitated initially, but replied, 'I want to be with somebody I love, and who loves me. A simple, happy family is all I wish for.'

'What about money, the luxuries?'

'I do not care much about them. A person may be rich, successful and even famous, but if he has nobody to share life's little joys and sorrows with, what is the point of having such luxuries?'

It was as if a cloud had lifted off Hitesh's mind. She was right.

Sensing it was quite late, they both went downstairs. Hitesh badly needed sleep; he had stayed up the previous four nights, worrying about the scam, or trying to not think of Sushma. He dozed off minutes after he lay on the bed.

It was seven in the morning and Hitesh was still sleeping. Payal woke him up with a smile and a cup of tea in her hands. 'Got to leave for office in an hour,' she said.

CHAPTER 23

Day 5

Hitesh was fending off fresh allegations every day, and putting out fires in different directions. The company was going to the dogs. Three franchisees had thrown in the towel; Super Cabs' manager in the North was roughed up by goons, sent by the Delhi franchisees, and he had quit the company; five other employees had put in their papers; two had decided not to show up since the controversy hit the roof. The rest soldiered on, supporting him through the crisis.

Mehta, on the other hand, was having a harrowing time after the chief minister summoned him. SEBI had sent in their officers to investigate the books of the company, while the Company Affairs Department and the income tax authorities were set to come knocking on his door anytime.

Hitesh hung up after a long conversation with the franchise operator in Bhubaneshwar, who, surprisingly, sounded sympathetic. He then turned on the television again.

SNB Business
The investor sentiment is still affected by reports of insider trading and the explosive story of a scam by the absconding CEO Venugopal Reddy, who is reportedly hiding in Toronto. SEBI is ready to probe the past annual reports of the company, and investigate into the authenticity of the numbers. The role of the advisors to the issue, Smith and Donald partners, and the bankers to the issue, RGV Bank, is currently being investigated. Mr Mehta,

CFO of the tainted company, says they will fully cooperate and respect any decisions.

IBS 360

It has come to light that Super Cabs is owned by a shell company, with a post office account in Channel Islands, through a series of shell companies set up in various parts of the globe. It is still unknown who owns this mysterious company. Can G.S. Rao, the former education minister, who is in hibernation at his Whitefield farmhouse in Bangalore, or the once-hailed future business leader Hitesh Patel, tell us?

News 7*24

The strike at Supreme Motors continues, in what seems to be a growing embarrassment, for the ruling coalition partners. The Opposition claims to have the support of five MLAs of G.S. Rao's maligned party, thanks to his involvement in the scam. While some franchisees claim its business as usual for them, and hope that the deadlock would be resolved soon, some are furious, and are contemplating legal action against Mr Hitesh Patel and Super Cabs.

K News

It is reported that there have been clashes between taxi drivers of the Operators' Union who ply taxis as per the token system and the drivers from the Super Cabs franchise in Chandigarh. The recent controversy has emboldened the local taxi drivers, who allege that Super Cabs is cutting into their business and preventing them from earning their livelihood. The ruling party MLA in Haryana has expressed his support to the local taxi drivers and has stated that shady businesses backed by black money and slush funds from abroad such as Super Cabs need to be investigated.

Bangalore Reporter

A former cab driver of the much-talked-about Super Cabs has made revelations regarding certain practices deployed by the company. He claims that the operator is a front for a prominent figure in the real estate industry, who runs various illegal businesses on the side, including drug peddling, dodgy nightclubs, a prostitution ring and a betting racket that rakes in millions. He claims that drivers were at the behest of the managers and fixers of these various rackets, and were made to support these operations in the city. The ruling coalition, known to be close to this mafia operator, has refuted these allegations, and the operator claims that the cab driver had previously been fired for showing up to work in an inebriated state. Who is speaking the truth?

Gurgaon Gazette

Super Cabs, once a poster child of entrepreneurship by the youth, is well on its path to become one of the greatest corporate fraud stories in India, with some beginning to call it Sleazy Cabs. A prominent journalist and blogger has advised women and families to steer clear of these cabs driven by crude and uncouth drivers, who are often under the influence of drugs. Three cases have been filed against the company and its operator in the past two months on various counts, the latest being the assault on a young student who was taking a cab home from the airport.

Payal knocked on his door, stirring Hitesh out of his deep thoughts.

'Hitesh, the police have entered the building along with some other government officers,' she said, sounding rushed.

Hitesh's troubles were growing by the minute. He walked out and met them near the elevator. He followed them quietly out of the office. On the way, a policeman informed him that Sahil, and the partner of Smith and Donald, Mr B.S. Somappa, had also been taken in for questioning.

Hitesh kept his head down as he was led through the frenzy of bite-hungry reporters and flashbulbs towards an unmarked van that whisked him away to the police station.

During his four hours of questioning, he repeatedly denied any involvement with Venu Reddy to participate in insider trading and in building up Super Cabs with the aim to raise its stock value and offload Reddy's interest. He remained firm that Super Cabs had long-term interests, and its workings and systems, could be probed to prove so. He was grilled for over an hour over the finances he had audited for Supreme Motors; here he appeared a bit nervous, and admitted to being soft, but stated firmly that all the working papers of his findings were handed over to the senior manager and partner, who then took a softer view, in the interest of their own billings in the future, and business relationship with Venu Reddy.

After a long wait in the interrogation room with Somappa and Sahil, who refused to look at him, all three were allowed to leave, but with a stern warning that they could not leave the city without legal permission.

An exhausted Hitesh returned to the office, and saw Payal waiting for him, along with his key staff.

'Mehta has had a stroke. He collapsed outside the office building while fielding questions on mafia links with the company. He's been rushed to the City Hospital...' Sukanya said.

'Oh my God! He's a bit too old to deal with this mess.'

'I got a call from Supreme Motors. There's news that the state government is bringing in industry veteran, Gopal Naidu, to take over the company and represent investor interests. The board members have been found to be inept, and seen as having glossed over all the reports. They are also being removed from other entities they represent: industry bodies, banks, business schools and other positions,' Payal said.

'There has to be some way to end this; we can't go on like this,' Hitesh said, before turning his attention to the television screen again.

IBS 360

Breaking News: The lockdown continues at the factory of Supreme Motors, where a minor scuffle broke out a few minutes ago between the riot police and embattled workers. Meanwhile the CPA Board has suspended the license to practice for Somappa and Sahil, who have been fired by Smith & Donald, the leading accounting and audit firm of the country. A panel constituted for the same is discussing charges against Hitesh Patel, and he is likely to meet a similar fate, although he still holds on to his position as the CEO of the troubled Super Cabs.

Hitesh received a frantic call from his mother who believed that he had been arrested. 'There are reporters standing outside the building, Hitesh. Shuklaji, our neighbour for over twenty years, created a ruckus today, telling your father that he has spoilt a respectable society. His condition has just worsened, beta.'

'I will pick both of you soon, Ma. You will stay at my apartment with Payal for a couple of days, till this storm blows over,' he said, picking up his keys, and gesturing to everyone that they were done for the day. 'Okay, Hitesh. But… Don't panic. God will set everything right soon. Whatever the world says, we are with you,' his mother said and hung up. Hitesh stood speechless for a while. The cameras flashed away as he and Payal drove out from the office, towards his home in Himayatnagar, the home he had left eighteen months ago.

'How is Mr Mehta? Is there any word from the hospital about his recovery?' he asked Payal on the way.

'I hear he's still in the ICU, but they say he's stable. But… his left arm and leg are paralysed.'

'Poor man,' Hitesh said as he turned into the lane on the dimly lit street.

CHAPTER 24

Day 10

Hitesh convened a meeting with Mahinder and Sohail, following the developments after his meeting with Gopal Naidu, the administrator in-charge of cleaning up the mess at Supreme Motors. Sukanya, who was pregnant, had taken a day off to keep away from the stress.

Hitesh explained to them that he had planned to pay back the Bangalore, Chennai and Mysore franchisees for vehicles that the company was unable to deliver as hitherto promised. He had managed to convince Gopal Naidu to find the cash, and remit these amounts to Super Cabs. He also stated his intention to discuss and reach a compromise with the head of a franchisee operation, which operated four franchises in the North. The collapse of three franchises in the previous week meant that the company was left with fifteen centres to operate from, and the intention was to hold on to all of them, till they could find a suitable buyer.

Payal sent him an SOS text asking him to turn on the television. Hitesh stood before the screen looking jaded, and wondered what more awaited him; his bank transactions were being investigated and trailed daily, and he was receiving a volley of abuses and threats from the franchise operators in the North, as well as from his old friend, Sahil.

IBS 360

It has come to light that Super Cabs had quite a controversial approach to choosing their franchisees. Mr Yadav, a tour operator in Kanpur, who applied for the Noida and Ghaziabad franchise, recounts a horror story. He was summoned to a five-star hotel where the company's then COO, Varun Rao, was put up. Over a round of drinks, he was asked to pay Rs 1 crore under the table, or forget about his chances of winning the bid. Yadav was unable to fork up the hefty bribe and the franchise was given to a roads contractor, whose father-in-law is a bureaucrat. We wonder if every franchise was negotiated in this manner. If so, where has all this money gone? Mr Varun Rao could not be contacted, and is said to have left the country too.

Hitesh cursed himself under his breath and switched the channel. All the while he had had a hunch that something was wrong with the way contracts were being negotiated and signed in his absence, but he couldn't put his finger on it back then.

News 7*24

The strike at Supreme Motors continues, and ruling coalition partners are growing increasingly nervous over the impasse. The Opposition claims to now have the support of seven MLAs of G.S. Rao's party. Venu Reddy is yet to be traced, although sources in the Foreign Ministry say that efforts are on to extradite him from Canada.

K News

Our correspondent R. Murthy, who is currently standing outside Hyderabad City Hospital, says that Sunil Mehta has gained consciousness, and has been talking to the police and other government-appointed investigators. We are being told that he constantly named Hitesh Patel as being behind the idea of setting up Super Cabs, along with Venu Reddy, and has denied any wrongdoing on his part.

Z News

The CPA Board has disqualified Hitesh Patel from the membership of its chapter, and has accused him of gross misrepresentation based on the investigations carried out. He gets a ban to practise as a CPA for life, while his former bosses at Smith & Donald have received a ten-year suspension from professional practice. The Company Affairs Department has also blacklisted Hitesh Patel, and has barred him from representation on the board of any company.

Hitesh's world came tumbling down. 'I've just received a text message from a reporter that the police will be coming here this afternoon. They have a clearance to arrest you,' Sohail said, looking at his phone. Payal, who had come into the cabin, moved to put her arms around Hitesh who was visibly disturbed.

'Boss, escape from here. You shouldn't be here when they come. Leave in my car; even if there are reporters outside, my car isn't the one they'll train their cameras on,' Mahinder said.

'But why should I run away? Let the law take its course.'

'Boss, get away for now. There's a lot of intrigue and politics involved. Right now, you haven't been summoned by the police. Just leave the city and the state. We'll work out some jugaad,' Mahinder said.

'I'm leaving with you,' Payal said in a tone of finality, putting an arm around his shoulder.

Hitesh was surprised. 'Don't be crazy, Payal. You're not serious, are you? I'm fleeing the city, and you want to run away with me? Stay here, and stay out of trouble.'

'No arguments. I'm leaving with you.' She held his hand in hers and looked at him intensely.

'Take her along; it will be a good cover for you. You'll be like a married couple and there will be less suspicion,' Mahinder said.

'But where do we get away to?'

'Let's go to Bhubaneshwar,' Payal suggested and everyone turned to look at her.

'What?' she said as the stares made her uncomfortable. 'I've got a friend there. Besides, this is past Vizag. They wouldn't imagine that you'd drive towards Vizag. They're likely to patrol roads towards Bangalore, Chennai and Mumbai.'

Aditya thought for a moment. He then packed his bag in a rush, taking a couple of files and a dossier of emails with him. 'Let's go. Let's not waste any time.'

'Here are my keys and my bank debit card; you know the password for the ATM. It's my son's date of birth, two days after yours. Don't use your cards; it can be traced by the authorities,' Mahinder warned as he handed him the things.

'Here's a SIM card, boss. I'll top it up this evening. Use this instead of your personal line; it's a prepaid line I used to call my brother in Riyadh,' Sohail said.

'We know the number, and will call or text you through a secure line,' Mahinder added. Hitesh was overwhelmed by their support, but had no time to thank anyone. Followed by Payal, he rushed out of the cabin and walked swiftly towards the elevator.

'I can't believe we're doing this. We're running away...' a confused Hitesh said, on the way to the parking spot.

'We have no option, Hitesh. Let's just go.' Hitesh slid into the backseat, squatting on all fours on the mat between the front and the backseat, while Payal slid into the driver's seat, and quickly reversed the silver Santro.

She nervously drove it out of the parking lot, and noticed three cameramen standing lazily, chatting outside the building. She drove past them without attracting attention. It seemed like the police had tipped them off on Hitesh's impending arrest. They stopped at her apartment for a few minutes, when she packed a duffel bag quickly. She also stuffed in it her father's trousers and a few of her brother's T-shirts for Hitesh, while he waited in the car.

A few minutes later, they were on NH9, heading towards their destination. They halted briefly for dinner late that night, 150 km before Behrampur. Hitesh then took over the wheels, and drove through most of the night. They arrived in Bhubaneshwar at 4.30 a.m. Payal's friend, Suchitra, had been intimated about their arrival from a phone booth near Vijayawada. As they stopped, they found Suchitra standing at the door; she had been giving instructions over the phone on how to reach her place. The two entered her apartment and collapsed on the bed, and continued to sleep till late in the evening.

CHAPTER 25

Day 17

Hitesh sat near the window the next morning, a cup of steaming tea in hand. He realized how this simple tea was a luxury for him, given the dramatic unfolding of events in his life over the past two weeks. He thought of his parents, especially his mother's last words, just before he ran away from Hyderabad like a fugitive. He hoped Mahinder had informed them of his whereabouts. Suddenly, a wave of hope and determination swept through him. He had to fight back, for the sake of his parents who loved him unconditionally, for the sake of his staff who had supported him in his ordeal, and for the sake of Payal, who had shown such trust in him. Did she love him? Hitesh, however, was too hurt to trust and love again.

He shivered for a moment as Payal came calling him to watch the news on the television. He felt awkward as he sat down to hear the media bark out all kinds of allegations against him. Payal handed him the remote, while Suchitra played with her toddler son. Her husband, Sumit, who did not seem too happy to have Hitesh in his house, was thankfully off to work.

Hitesh anxiously switched channels, looking for any news on the situation at Supreme Motors. To his relief, the news that had occupied centre-stage was that the government was in a difficult position, and was being called to prove its majority. The ruling party's high command had sent union ministers as emissaries to try and sort out the situation.

IBS 360

In what appears to be the latest on the Supreme Motors scam, former minister G.S. Rao has been admitted in Bangalore Central Hospital, as he had been complaining of chest pain. Over the past few days, he was visited by investigators who spent long hours going through his finances, and grilled him on his role and involvement in the set up of Super Cabs.

(The spokesperson for G.S. Rao speaking into the camera): 'Saar has been cooperating with the authorities. He is under a lot of stress with his name being dragged into the mud. The real culprits are absconding, and should be found and punished.'

Meanwhile, Venugopal Reddy and Hitesh Patel remain untraceable, and the authorities are looking for these once hailed executives.

Hitesh wondered if he had done the right thing by leaving, but realized that it could have been a risk to stay. He switched channels.

*News 7*24*

The Opposition claims that they now have the support of ten MLAs of G.S. Rao's maligned party, and are likely to pass a motion for the government to prove its majority. In another move, the state finance minister has appointed R.G. Somaraju, the former MD of Hyderabad Bank, as the administrator of Super Cabs. He has been given the task of finding a buyer for the beleaguered cab service, as it hops from one challenge to another. In other news, the Reddy family, which owned twenty per cent of Supreme Motors, has transferred its stake to a Worker's Cooperative Group, in a move to reach out to workers, and make them feel invested in the company. The workers will now own twenty per cent of the company, and will be able to earn dividend as well as see their interests better represented at the board level. Although they're yet to call off the strike, it is learnt that the workers were jubilant about this, and most were keen to go back to work. Mohan Babu, the leader, however, played down this effort to reach out to workers. He said that a full disclosure on the findings of the conspiracy against the workers is necessary, and all their demands must be met. It's unclear what further demands they have at this stage.

K News

Sunil Mehta has claimed that he played no part in setting up Super Cabs, nor did he benefit from it in anyway. He claims that Hitesh Patel is the key to all answers, and hopes that the authorities take him into custody. G.V. Vinod, the HR manager, who was beaten up at the Supreme Motors facility a few weeks ago, was given a hero's welcome by the workers today. After being fed sweets by Mohan Babu and garlanded by the workers, he said that his priority is to work out a compromise between the new management and the workers.

Z News

The authorities are still on the lookout for Hitesh Patel who has fled from the city. Many of his friends, colleagues and neighbours are shocked at the recent turn of events. Most people know him as a soft-spoken, hard-working and good-natured individual. Sources we spoke to have good things to say about him and his work, and find the allegations against him to be shocking. His parents have left Hyderabad for Baroda this evening, where, the neighbours say, they have a house and a few close relatives. The parents claim that they are unaware of his whereabouts. Hitesh is likely to be tried in court on various counts that include fraud, professional misconduct and collusion in addition to, as unnamed sources have learnt, charges of insider trading and misrepresentation.

In the evening, Hitesh called Mahinder from his prepaid card on a number that was texted to him a while back.

'Sir, there are people coming in everyday. Some major audit of everything we've done is going on. I was questioned for two hours on your whereabouts; luckily, no one noticed you take my car.'

'How is the situation in office? How's the staff holding up? The franchisees?'

'The staff is being questioned about their knowledge of your location. Everyone is worried about you, sir. I would suggest you leave and move to a quieter place. Don't take any risk…'

'I want to come back, Mahinder. This won't work. It will only get worse,' Hitesh chimed in.

'Your return has to be negotiated, boss. Don't worry; you're not a hardened criminal. The guys are politely asking their questions and getting no answers. But you better move; it's not safe staying in one place.'

'I haven't left the apartment since I came. Only Payal has gone out a couple of times.'

'Still you must consider moving to another place. Meanwhile, I'll get ready to welcome Somaraju tomorrow.'

'Okay. Thanks, Mahinder. Keep me updated.'

Hitesh walked to Payal with a grave expression on his face. 'We need to move; it isn't safe here anymore. Any suggestions on where we could go?'

Sumit turned in Hitesh's direction, putting down his newspaper. 'Hmm… Leave right away then. You can go to Damanjodi; it's quiet and safe. Also, given the presence of a PSU, there'll be less suspicion. You'll come across as a couple who's just moved.'

'How do we get there?' Hitesh asked, looking at a newspaper article that had caught his eyes: there was speculation that G.S. Rao had been cozying up to Ranga Naidu, in an attempt to destabilize the ruling alliance.

'Hirakand Express. It leaves at 8 p.m. Both of you have an hour to reach the railway station. I know somebody there, a very good friend, who lives in a nice area in a big, independent house. I'll call him after I drop you off at the station. You could stay there for a couple of days.'

CHAPTER 26

Day 23

Hitesh returned to the house after a short run in the park nearby. With his cap and a twenty-day-old beard, he was barely recognizable. Payal was helping Mrs Bhatia in the kitchen. She had grown close to Mrs Bhatia and the two children. The Bhatias, both employees at NALCO, had taken them in considerately, without many questions.

Hitesh spent most of the day following the news, while Payal cooked for them and solved crossword puzzles in the free time. They had also spent some time together over the last few days, taking walks and exploring the little town at the foot of the hills.

Hitesh entered the kitchen and handed them a few items of grocery that Payal had requested him to bring. Hitesh remained inside and stared at Payal. She was looking different, though he could not immediately make out what it was. Then he realized that she had kept her hair open, which she usually didn't. It fell over her shoulders and the back carelessly. Little beads of sweat had appeared on her forehead as she stirred something in a vessel placed on the gas stove. She looked angelic. Hitesh could not help but compare her with Sushma. Sushma was pretty, no doubt, but Payal's beauty was raw, earthy. She gave him a questioning look.

'Do you want to get some fresh air?' he asked her.

Payal hesitated. 'Go on, Payal. Take a break. Once the kids are back from their friend's house, they won't leave you alone,' Mrs Bhatia said.

'Alright, let's go,' she said.

They walked quietly for a while. Hitesh slowly took her hand in his and massaged it softly. They stopped at a little tea stall, a short distance from the community park.

'What's in the news today?' she asked, worried about his disturbed state of mind. Hitesh had become quite temperamental of late; on some days he was irritable, on others apologetic.

'Mixed signals. One news channel talked about how the company has found a buyer, a mid-sized auto components firm. On another side, selling off Super Cabs to the group of remaining franchisees is being considered. Most of them are doing good business. Venu Reddy is suspected to be in Montreal, and the government is planning for his arrest. Apparently, they're stepping up efforts for my search, as if I'm some dangerous criminal.'

'Hmm... Don't worry, Hitesh. But yes, the police should be after more important issues like the Naxalite struggle and murders in the city. Anyway, it's positive news regarding Supreme Motors. The franchisees taking over Super Cabs isn't too bad, is it?'

'I imagine so; at least most of the franchisees understand the business. Do you know that I am now being accused of receiving money in appointing some of the franchisees?'

Payal sighed. 'Don't worry; the truth will come to light soon. Have you spoken to Mahinder or Sohail?'

'I did, a couple of days back. They haven't been able to approach any important person in the ministry yet. They need to catch the right people in the government to push through a deal.'

'It will happen. I have full faith in you,' she said, resting her head on his shoulders. The waiter served them a plate of pakoras with masala tea, putting a break to the conversation about Super Cabs. Both silently ate for a while.

'I think you trust me a little too much, Payal. To an extent, I'm at fault here. I glossed over certain facts that I could, and should have been more careful about. I knew that G.S. Rao had funded the business. During the time when Venu was undermining my authority, giving undue liberty to Varun to take decisions, I had a hunch about what he was up to, but failed to act upon it.'

Payal looked at him intently. 'We all have our reasons that guide our actions, and we all make compromises; you made yours, and you've learned from it.'

'The reasons were self-interest. I took up the job because it paid more, and held on to it because I was building something new, and had a major responsibility.'

'That is fine, right? That's what any person with your intellect and capability would have done.'

'Actually no. I mucked around; I knew some of the things going on around me were wrong. I was fully aware that Super Cabs was set up by Venu to save his own skin. The reason why I helped him do it was that my life sucked. I was a small-time accountant who worked for more than sixteen hours a day and earned peanuts. My social life was non-existent, and I was bitter and frustrated to see other people's success, both in their personal as well as professional lives. Venu's offer showed me the money and the high life, and I got carried away.'

'I know, Hitesh. Though we never talked, I have noticed your transformation from a simple, hard-working accountant to a star in the corporate world. You did what it takes to be successful, but you are still a much better person than Mehta or Venu Reddy. I've seen what they're made of; they deserve what's coming to them. As far as you are concerned, we'll find a way out for you.' Hitesh nodded his head, and she gazed at him with affection.

'Thank you, Payal,' he said meekly.

'Don't,' she said, gesturing to him to say no more. They sat silently, holding hands.

'By the way, you look beautiful with your hair let loose.'

'Oh, really?' she blushed. She lowered her eyes, smiling. 'So you noticed.'

Hitesh smiled. He remembered how, with Sushma, he would immediately notice even the minor things. The nail colour she had applied, or the way she styled her hair. With Payal, he would converse for hours but was never bothered about her clothes or appearance. He was always attentive in Sushma's presence, constantly trying to do things the way it pleased her best, but, with Payal he could be himself, effortlessly. Her smile brightened him and her words put him at ease.

His phone rang; it was Deepak Bhatia, the gentleman they were living with. Hitesh picked up the phone and listened to him quietly; his calm expression turned into a frown.

He hung up and turned to Payal, who looked at him quizzically.

'We need to leave tonight. The kid who lives down the street and comes over to Bhatia's to play has told his mum that he's seen you on TV. Fortunately, he didn't know on which channel. His mum just called up Mrs Bhatia, asking if you were a television actress. Mrs. Bhatia laughed it off saying that she didn't know, though you look like one. Now, this lady's brother is the local inspector.'

'Oh my God! That kid has such sharp eyes! Luckily for us, your beard is a good disguise. It's better not to take chances; we must go somewhere else. But where will we go?'

Hitesh thought hard. 'Let me text Rajesh, my friend. He might help.' After a furious exchange of messages, Hitesh looked up with a smile.

'His sister and brother in-law are in Ranchi. He says we can go and stay with them. There's a train to Jamshedpur tonight at 2 a.m. Their house is a couple of hours' drive from that station. Rajesh is booking tickets for us in his name, and will send those to me by email soon.'

Payal laughed at their strange situation. 'The adventure continues,' she chuckled. 'Let's go,' she said, taking his hand.

'You're having fun, is it?' he asked, looking very tensed himself.

'This gives me a chance to spend more and more time with you; of course I'm having fun,' she gushed. Hitesh smiled.

'Alright. Let's keep moving. We won't stop till Mahinder has worked something out. I've never been to Jamshedpur or Ranchi; let's see where it takes us,' he said as they walked back to the Bhatia residence. It had begun to grow dark, and the dim street bulbs gave the neighbourhood a dull glow. There were few people on the road, apart from the stray dogs that ran amok, lunging at each other for scraps of food near the dustbin. The moonlit sky wore a deep shade of purple and was partially covered with dark grey clouds.

CHAPTER 27

Day 25

Mohan Babu sat back, and rubbed his palm over his belly, a toothpick in his mouth. He belched loudly and smiled to himself before wiping the sweat on the forehead and bald patch with a handkerchief. He adjusted the several gold rings on his fingers, and smiled to himself again. Suresh smoked a cigarette and lecherously gazed at the bar dancer gyrating to Bollywood numbers on the other side of the bar. G.V. Vinod, an arm in a cast, also had his eyes set on her ample bosom, enjoying the change from his mundane existence.

'So the company will be sold, that's what you're saying?' Suresh asked Mohan Babu.

'It's a done deal; it will be announced very soon. They'll keep old-timers like Vinod and me, for six months and retire us with a VRS package,' Mohan Babu said lethargically.

'I'd rather retire here than go and retire in Hyderabad. They are offering us a handsome compensation package,' Vinod said.

'True, and we've had our revenge too, haven't we? We have become heroes after exposing Venugopal and that mouse Hitesh. G.S. Rao is in a predicament, and had come to meet Naidu Garu. He wants to topple the government, after they survived the trust vote by a whisker. He still has twelve MLAs in his hand. And the CM isn't keen to take him in as a minister till the charges are cleared. He has negotiated with Naidu Garu to become the labour minister,' Mohan Babu said, ecstatic.

'This is explosive! So G.S. Rao, who we got in trouble, will now join Ranga Naidu and topple the government! Amazing! What's in it for you?' Suresh asked.

'The party will endorse my name for mayor in our district. Elections are to happen in six months. I've spoken to the party about both of you. Suresh, you can join the party as the treasurer; your ideas will help us. Vinod, you can be the party spokesperson for Vizag and the surrounding region. We needed someone smart and respectable, who could speak to the media. I recommended your name.'

'Thank you, Babu Sir.' Vinod looked pleased and picked up his pint of beer with his good hand.

Suresh smiled from ear to ear. 'I'm happy to work for the party, but I'll be happier to be put in a behind-the-scenes position, where I'm not seen, only heard.' He grinned in Vinod's direction before lighting up another cigarette.

'What do you think will happen to the case?' Vinod asked, while watching the dancer as she gyrated to the tune of *Kajra re*.

'As long as Venu Reddy and Hitesh are absconding, they're presumed guilty. Once they're arrested, they're in deep trouble,' Suresh said with a wicked laugh. He had drunk more than his normal capacity, and his speech was slurred.

'That fellow Hitesh is dangerous, and too clever. I have tipped off some policemen who are loyal to Naidu Garu. Once we're in power and he is caught, we'll kill the bastard. We can make it look like he was trying to escape, but got shot in an encounter. Venu Reddy has too many demons to battle; his own family has turned against him,' Mohan Babu sniggered.

'True, and without G.S. Rao's backing, his films are stuck,' Suresh said. He got up from the chair and walked across to the manager of the bar. After an animated negotiation, he returned.

'I need money, Mohan Babu. About Rs 20,000 will do for now,' Suresh said carefully.

'Here, take Rs 50,000,' Mohan Babu said, pulling out a wad of 1,000-rupee notes, and thumping it on the table. 'It's a gift from Naidu Garu. After all, you're part of the party now,' he smiled. 'Yours will reach your home tomorrow,' he told Vinod, who appeared calm, but was gulping down his drinks quickly.

'I will take your leave then,' Suresh said, before stumbling out through the back door. Moments later, the bar dancer, with her gaudy make-up, garish saree and clanking heels, hurried out behind him.

■

Hitesh closed the book and lay in the bed pondering over where they would run away to next. Payal was fast asleep next to him. They were making efforts to keep a low profile. They went out only early in the morning or after dark, staying out of sight from the Ojha family's neighbours. It had been four days and he realized that they had overstayed their visit to Ranchi. The Ohjas lived in a small apartment, and the children's bedroom was given to Hitesh and Payal, while the kids slept in the tiny living room. He had noticed that they were getting restless as the days passed, as if they missed their space. He stood near the window and watched the nightlights in the town, blurred by thick drops of rain that had begun a short while ago.

He turned on his laptop and connected it to the internet cable. Mahinder had promised to email him about the efforts he was making to reach someone high up in the ministry. But before he signed in to the new email account he had created, he opened the website of *Hyderabad Reporter* to see the latest news.

Hyderabad Reporter
The beleaguered Super Cabs was sold today to a group of its franchisees at an undisclosed price. The government aims to use the receipts for community development and the investor's protection

fund, managed by the Securities Board. Mr Naik, CEO of the newly formed company, Super Fleet, said that the services would be re-branded as 800-CABS, and the fleet would be painted yellow as opposed to the current dull green. This will give the company a new identity to forge a better future on, he said. Meanwhile, Supreme Motors, which has nearly been acquired by a components major, would be calling off the employees' strike, after the worker's demand for a ten to fifteen per cent increment was accepted by the new owners. The workers also own twenty per cent of the company shares, transferred to them by the Reddy family. Deliveries to the newly formed 800-CABS and other pending orders are expected to be cleared very soon. However, the search for the former chiefs of these companies, Venu Reddy and Hitesh Patel, continues.

Hitesh then read the email he had received from Mahinder:

Boss, situation within the government is tense. G.S. Rao is blackmailing and threatening to withdraw support. Supreme Motors and Super Cabs have been sold off, so he almost doesn't care now. The ruling alliance is scampering to save the government. Anyway, I'll try something in a couple of days. I'm discretely circulating some of the evidence you had passed on. I hope this works. Hope Payal and you are in good spirits.

Hitesh replied to him:

Thanks for all your help. Payal is very patient. I couldn't have managed without her. Please try everything you can; this whole thing is getting very stressful and tiring. Hope the staff is fine and happy with the takeover.

CHAPTER 28

Day 30

Hitesh paced up and down in the room in anticipation of a call from Mahinder. He had been irritable all day, sniping even at Payal. This was partly due to the torrential rain for the past couple of days that had forced them to be locked up inside. The host family was away: the kids were in school and the parents at work. Payal was preparing lunch when he turned on the television.

K News

Hitesh Patel is again in the line of fire with another shocking allegation, this time by an ex-female colleague. Sandra De'mello, an intern who worked with Smith & Donald a year ago, has accused the absconding former CEO of Super Cabs of sexual exploitation. She claims that he had taken MMS clips of her and her boyfriend in compromising positions, and forced her to get intimate with him, threatening and blackmailing her if his requests were not complied with. She claims that he used to call her during late hours of the night, and harass her during the course of an assignment. G.V. Vinod, HR manager of Supreme Motors, claims that her allegations are true, and he had seen Hitesh trying to get intimate with the young woman on many occasions, during an audit visit to Vizag. In a statement from prison, Sahil, Hitesh's former boss, who is serving a sentence, also admits to receiving a complaint from her regarding sexual harassment charges. This follows a shocking allegation made by a small-time model and actress, Sushma Raghavan, a week ago, that she was harassed by Hitesh for sexual favours, and wasn't even paid for the Super Cabs advertisement that she had done at his behest. It seems like Hitesh Patel's troubles aren't going to go away anytime soon.

Hitesh sat stoned. Payal came in from the kitchen and sat down quietly next to him. He looked at her but she turned her gaze away.

'Are you mad at me? Payal, all this is a lie. It was Vinod and Suresh who had shot the MMS clip of hers and not me, in fact, I had stopped the clip from reaching the management. All this is motivated. You know that the allegations by Sushma aren't true either.'

'Just keep quiet, Hitesh! Just stop talking.' Payal brushed his arm away as he tried to hold her hand.

'I don't understand how you can believe any of this. I didn't…' Hitesh spoke again.

'I know the truth, Hitesh. But you were stupid enough to get involved with these tramps and gold diggers. I'm irritated with you for being a fool and getting trapped by such people.' Hitesh looked stung by her rebuke. He silently changed the channel.

CHAPTER 29

Payal hadn't spoken much to him since morning. She was moving from room to room gathering things and putting them in their right place, while attending to the kitchen in between. Hitesh wondered if she was still angry at the allegations made against him by Sushma and Sandra. Whatever it was, her silence was troubling him. The Bhatias had left for a relative's place an hour ago, and would be home shortly. Hitesh had something to tell Payal. He kept following her wherever she went, but she appeared in no mood to talk.

Finally, he gathered courage and stopped her by grabbing her hand.

'What?' she asked.

'Why aren't you talking to me?'

'I have just been busy. You can see that.'

'You can do this later. I want to talk to you,' he looked her straight in the eye.

She felt uncomfortable. 'What is it?' she asked cautiously.

'Come and sit down first,' he led her to the sofa holding her hand.

Payal was surprised. 'Tell me fast. Has anything happened? I haven't watched the news since morning.'

Hitesh smiled. 'You were angry with me a moment ago and now, you are so concerned.'

She looked away in reply.

'You seem upset with me. You are disturbed by the allegations made against me by Sushma and Sandra, aren't you?'

'Yes I am,' she answered sternly.

'I promise I wouldn't be so stupid again to get involved with these shameless gold diggers.' He smiled mischievously as Payal sat puzzled. Then she remembered her own words and gave a mock frown. 'It's your life, why should I bother?' she said, looking serious and averting her gaze from his.

'I want you to bother, and I need you to keep me in check,' he said, the grin intact. 'I love you. It's taken me a while to realize that, but I do. Will you marry me, Payal?' Hitesh asked, now serious.

Payal sat shocked into stillness. Her eyes brightened and she broke into a smile. She then blushed and turned away from his burning gaze. For a while, he just stared at her lovingly while she sat with eyes lowered, smiling to herself. Finally, she looked up and nodded. 'Yes. Yes, Hitesh,' she said, her eyes moist and face pink.

'I am so happy, Payal. I'm glad to have you in my life. You have given me courage to fight, and a reason to carry on. I do not know what I would have done if it weren't for you. Just being with you makes me happy. I wish I could marry you right away,' he said and paused. 'Will you wait for me if they find me guilty, and send me to jail?'

'I wish you will come out clean, Hitesh. But whatever the verdict may be, I am with you. Let's fight the battle together. Just like we have been doing so far,' she replied calmly and put her arm around his neck.

'I love you, Payal,' he said and brought her closer to him before kissing her softly. The doorbell rang and they moved away, breaking into a laugh.

CHAPTER 30

Z News

We have been told that after a rather tense two-hour long meeting, former minister and APGC President G.S. Rao has withdrawn support from the ruling Liberal Democratic Alliance led by Chief Minister Ramsekar Reddy. The CM has accused G.S. Rao of blackmail, as he was not reinstated as a minister till the charges against him were cleared. His actions were termed as 'vindictive,' and he was accused of 'horse trading'. It is learnt that he has the support of seventeen MLAs including four independent MLAs, and he will be joining them in an alliance with the opposition leader Ranga Naidu, to stake claim to form the government. A no-confidence motion has been filed against the government, and the CM will have to prove his majority on the floor of the assembly in three days. The ruling alliance is understandably tense, and is likely to be defeated despite the good handling of the scam related to Supreme Motors. G.S. Rao confirmed talks with his arch rival Ranga Naidu, and promised to topple the government that was using fake allegations to frame him and sideline him from politics. Ranga Naidu says that he welcomes the respected G.S. Rao, a popular social worker, into their fold and dismissed allegations related to Supreme Motors as a conspiracy by the ruling party.

It was evening. Hitesh watched the news with bated breath. Just then, Mahinder's number flashed on his phone. He picked it up on the first ring.

'Call me back in five minutes. I'll have the CM's political secretary with me. If you can convince him, he'll put you through,'

Mahinder said before hanging up.

Ten minutes later, he was on a secure line, waiting to speak to the chief minister.

'Where are you? You've got us in enough trouble already,' the CM said, sounding irritable.

'Sir, I'm not responsible for what has been said and done. Let's talk about how I can help you. You have limited time…'

'What evidence do you have against G.S. Rao?'

'I have access to documents and bank transactions that trace back to him and his family. Shell companies were set up that owned Super Cabs through a web of transactions. These companies had expenses too: holidays abroad, purchase of properties, payment of college fees and living expenses of a student and many other interesting things. All these expenses are attributable to G.S. Rao and his immediate family. You can trace these back through passports that show entry and exit, and other documents.'

'Do you have these documents? Where did you get these?'

'Let's just say I have my sources,' he said, smiling at Payal, who put her hand on his. She had taken risks on several occasions to source those documents from Venu Reddy's files that she once had access to.

'Okay, hand these over and we could look at bringing you in as an informant and clearing you of all your charges.'

'That's not the way I'd like to do it, Reddy Sir. I want to clear my name. A lot of things have been said and done against me in the past month…'

'I'm not sure we are in a negotiating position here,' the CM said tersely.

'I have documents that can save your government, sir. Account numbers of banks where Venu Reddy has siphoned off whatever profit he made on the stock market. Also, I have evidence that will incriminate Mohan Babu, and those who stand with him in this whole scam.'

'He's the guy who led the protests, right?'

'Yes, he is. He is with Ranga Naidu's party and wants to contest elections. He's a ruthless man with political ambitions and damning secrets.'

'Hmm...What do you have in mind?'

Hitesh turned to Payal and smiled at her, giving her the thumbs up sign before he began.

CHAPTER 31

Day 32

IBS 360

Another dramatic turn of events: government has confirmed that Hitesh Patel was kept in a safe house in Bhadrachalam under police protection till all the evidence had been collected and investigated. Sources say that he has helped the police and various authorities in their investigation by providing them full cooperation and support. The state police swung into action this morning and, in a shocking move, have arrested G.S. Rao who, after being tipped off about his imminent arrest, was on his way to the hospital. The police arrested him before he entered Hyderabad City Hospital. Sunil Mehta, Mohan Babu, R.V. Suresh and G.V. Vinod were also arrested on various counts of fraud, misdemeanor, obstructing peace and inciting violence.

We have Hitesh Patel in our studio for an exclusive interview where he hopes to clear the air.

Reporter: 'Hitesh, who owned Super Cabs?'

Hitesh (pausing and smiling nervously): 'It was owned through a web of transactions on account of various shell companies. I don't know where the money came from, apart from being told once by Venu Reddy that G.S. Rao would be investing in this project. When we met for the first time, Rao was fully apprised of the business idea, and was totally in support of it, although I had no individual discussion with him. The company was set up and Mehta, who is now in police custody, handled the transactions.'

Reporter: 'Is there anything else that you're aware of which linked G.S. Rao to these transactions?'

Hitesh: 'I've handed documents to the authorities that show that these shell companies which invested in Super Cabs were also spending money abroad on holiday trips, leisure, spa and cosmetic treatments and education for G.S. Rao's family. If he had nothing to do with these shell companies, why were they picking up his tabs?'

Reporter: 'That's damning evidence. Where does Venu Reddy come in?'

Hitesh: 'Super Cabs was an exciting venture for me and it had many challenges. We had to grow and build something sustainable out of nothing. However, one of the limitations I had to deal with was being undermined by Varun Rao, who earned kickbacks. Venu Reddy was aggressively trying to grow Super Cabs in order to build business for Supreme Motors, and then sell out.

I've given the government all the details that will help them draw these funds back into the country, from bank accounts abroad. Venu Reddy was also a front for G.S. Rao and handled his investments, including film projects.'

Reporter: 'What roles have Mohan Babu, R.V Suresh and G.V. Vinod played in this recent agitation?'

Hitesh: 'A significant one. The whole thing was created at a time when Supreme Motors had begun doing well, and Mohan Babu was asked to leave, due to the allegations made in a respectable newspaper that he had conspired to murder a subordinate he didn't get along with. The reason he did it was because Supreme Motors was getting ready to hand over incriminating evidence based on an investigation they had carried out before the case came forth to the media. There are some emails with the authorities, who are looking into them. Suresh and Vinod, along with their accomplice Mohan Babu, are corrupt to the core. Again, the authorities have all the evidence based on the audit findings from a year ago.

Reporter: 'Mohan Babu called for a strike to protect workers' interest. That was his stated intention.'

Hitesh: 'I don't believe so. For years, these men robbed the company blindly, and it was on the brink of collapse. Last year, they had just about enough cash to meet a month's expenses. I helped them recover a significant sum from the likes of Suresh and Vinod, who were receiving kickbacks from purchase contracts, housing, scrap sales, and sale of defective vehicles. Mohan Babu was their godfather back then. Surely, he didn't think of the workers' interests then, did he?'

Reporter: 'What was your intention behind joining Super Cabs? There's an allegation that this was created for Venu Reddy to hike up share value and divest his stake...'

Hitesh: 'Surely that wasn't my intention. Starting a car rental company was a suggestion I gave to Venu Reddy when we got talking about the problems Supreme Motors was in. I was looking for a job then, as I was unhappy with my work and life at Smith & Donald. Venu made me a compelling offer, and I believed that it was the right thing to do. It was a challenge to build a new business, a great experience if you will. If you read the findings, you'll see that we had created something valuable; that's why franchisees came forward to buy into the company, having seen business value in what we had created.'

Reporter: 'Super Cabs had its share of problems...'

Hitesh: 'Its problems can be broken down into three. One created by the rapid expansion and wrong decisions by Varun Rao, who had the backing of Venu Reddy. He took several questionable decisions even when I wasn't involved, or didn't approve of them. The second was a result of the poor quality standards at Supreme Motors. Thirdly and lastly, being a new business, it had its own challenges, and there is always a learning curve. We invested in the right systems and people to overcome those.

Reporter: 'We have three more questions. You have been accused of glossing over the problems at Supreme Motors. Your response to this allegation?'

Hitesh: 'A very unfair accusation, that one. Yes, you can say I was optimistic about their future, given that Venu Reddy had taken steps to implement change. However, everything I saw and did was documented and signed off by my senior manager, Sahil, and the partner. It's possible that they made a few ethical adjustments for business development reasons. You'll see in the reports that I managed to uncover fraud that remained under the rug for ten years. You should also hold the board at Supreme Motors responsible. It doesn't seem they asked the management any questions. Although, in hindsight, maybe I should have discharged my duties independently, and not made a compromise.'

Reporter: 'Were you aware that Venu Reddy was pushing hard to divest from Supreme Motors?'

Hitesh: 'Yes and no. I knew he was aggressive on wanting us to grow Super Cabs, and this would in turn help Supreme Motors and its valuation. But I was unaware of any unfair means used to accomplish this objective. I worked eighty hours a week, with the sole focus of setting up Super Cabs as a sustainable business. Anyway, I've also given the authorities all the details, and helped them channel all the money that Venu Reddy made from the sale of shares of Supreme Motors, back into the country. I was entrusted to manage his offshore accounts, and do these transactions for him. Maybe I should have quit at that point, but my sense of duty towards my staff and franchisees prevented me from doing so.'

Reporter: 'Fair enough; let the investigating authorities judge that. What is your response to Sandra De'mello and Sushma's allegations against you?'

Hitesh: 'Where do I begin? Sandra has little morality and credibility. She's been fired from her last two jobs for misbehaviour, and I was told that she was fired from Smith & Donald too. She absconded from work all the time on different excuses. She was a disaster to work with; the less said about her the better. With Sushma, yes, there was intimacy. We've known each other from college and were in a relationship. The advertisement for Super Cabs was a starting point, and everyone from our marketing team to the creative agency approved of her doing it. We got a model for an endorsement for free, and she got a break. I don't know what she's going on about. I feel she is doing it for publicity, but there was no harassment at any point. Again, all of this is well set up by some political forces.'

Post Hitesh's interview, which gave a different light to the events that had transpired over the last forty days, the government swept into action by charge-sheeting Mohan Babu and the other accused men, R.V. Suresh, Mehta and G.V. Vinod. The CM won the trust vote the following day, aided by fifteen MLAs who had earlier supported G.S. Rao, but post Hitesh's expose, quickly shifted camps.

After months of courtroom drama, G.S. Rao was convicted for false declaration of assets, and sentenced to one year of imprisonment. Mohan Babu was convicted of planning and conspiring murder of a fellow worker at Supreme Cabs; inciting riots with the aim of damaging life and property; and above all, for fraud. He was sentenced to ten years of rigorous imprisonment. Mehta was sentenced to serve six months in jail for aiding fraud, while R.V. Suresh, G.V. Vinod and Varun Rao were sentenced to two years of imprisonment each. Venu Reddy, who was deported to India, was given a prison sentence of five years, while Hitesh Patel served a sentence of one year, guilty of misrepresenting the account books of Supreme Motors and professional misconduct. He was also ordered to undertake four years of community service soon after his imprisonment. Hitesh, Sahil and three local partners of Smith & Donald were barred from professional practice for life. The former board members of Supreme Motors were removed from all board positions they held, and were blacklisted.

Sushma, despite a few modelling assignments, and her desperate efforts to gain publicity through the scam, didn't make it too far and even struggled with substance abuse. She was reduced to a waitress at a cocktail bar in dusty Doha where she worked for a year. Later, she married a reporter who wrote for a small-time film magazine, and settled down to a quieter life, raising a family and ruing her missed opportunities.

Payal and Hitesh got married soon after his release from the prison, and moved to Baroda where Hitesh's parents now live. Hitesh began to manage an old-age home run by a Baroda-based NGO, while Payal took up a secretarial job in an office.

Rajesh did not face much trouble locating the house. The two-storied, old-style building, walls mildewed at places, stood at the end of a busy, dusty lane. The door opened and he saw Hitesh greet him with a smile. The two friends hugged each other and went inside. Payal soon came in, a tray holding a glass of water in hand. Hitesh's parents too came from their room and greetings were exchanged.

After a while, Rajesh, Hitesh and Payal sat in the main room talking about the good old days and the scam. Rajesh then opened his bag and handed Hitesh a file. 'Here are all your papers and documents,' he said. Hitesh looked satisfied while Payal gave a puzzled look.

Hitesh looked at Rajesh and they both grinned, looking at Payal, who was deeply perplexed. Hitesh began, 'You know, Payal, tomorrow I spend my last day at the NGO, and hence complete my sentence. You never asked what I will do after this. Well, here it is: we are leaving Baroda in a week to build a new life in Cyprus.'

'You can't be serious!' Payal blurted out.

'I am. We'll all are catching a train to Ahmedabad next week, and then flying out to Larnaca the same day.' Payal sat with surprise etched all over her face.

'There is only one secret that I have kept from you in all these years. Remember the time when Supreme Motors was trading at Rs 100 per share, and Venu Reddy wanted to drive the price up to Rs 150?' Payal nodded. 'Well, Rajesh, Sachin and I invested three crores in the market through various traders and firms owned by Rajesh's father and his immediate family. In two months, we made one-and-a-half-crores split three ways. Rajesh invested that money in the stock market over the past five years. It yielded a net value of one crore for my share, after adjusting market gains and losses. He made a trip to Cyprus last year, and got a plot booked in my name.'

'What?' Payal exclaimed, totally surprised. 'This is some news!'

Hitesh's father had walked into the room. He stood there with a frown on his face. 'But isn't this a rather crooked means to make money?' he asked sternly.

Hitesh sighed. 'Yes, you may say that. I did, but in a small way. I did what anyone would have done in my position. Don't people bribe the traffic cop to avoid paying fines, or understate returns to tax authorities? Don't businessmen and top executives splurge "business expenses" on holidays abroad? Even this is paltry compared to what people in power make, those who spend crores on a wedding, or who start out as "humble farmers", and soon own a Maybach or a Porsche. There is no limit to scams, be it the recent telecom scam or that related to hosting a major sporting event. Some of the richest people in the country never pay taxes. I could go on and on.

'All I wanted was an opportunity to carve a better life for me, a life considered a distant dream for simple folks like us. I now have that opportunity. It's time to move on; I've made up for my wrongdoings and paid my dues. By now, Hitesh Patel is a forgotten man. There are bigger scams to unearth and bigger fishes to catch. And, Papa, don't forget I've done a bit of good too. I've saved a company which was on a brink of collapse, and started a new business that created jobs. I even prevented the last government from being voted out.'

His father shrugged his shoulders and grunted in approval. Payal too relaxed a little. The last five years had been hard on the family. They had to swallow a bitter pill and rebuild their lives.

Rajesh laughed while the look of bewilderment on Payal's face changed into a smile. After his father left the room, she hurled a cushion at Hitesh in mock anger. 'So much for my creative ideas,' Hitesh said, returning the smile, and looking lovingly at his six months' pregnant wife. They couldn't wait to begin a new life, together.